Amin Maalouf is a Lebanese journalist and writer. He was formerly director of the weekly international edition of the leading Beirut daily *an-Nahar*, and editor-in-chief of *Jeune Afrique*. He now lives with his wife and three children in Paris. Amin Maalouf's previous novels, *Leo the African*, *Samarkand* (winner of the *Prix des maisons de la presse*, *The Gardens of Light* and *The Rock of Tanios* (winner of the *Prix Goncourt*) are all available in Abacus paperback.

Dorothy S. Blair has published translations of many books written in French, in addition to writing original critical works.

'Maalouf's novels recreate the thrill of childhood reading, that primitive mixture of learning about something unknown or unimagined and forgetting utterly about oneself.'

Guardian

Also by Amin Maalouf

LEO THE AFRICAN
SAMARKAND
THE ROCK OF TANIOS
THE GARDENS OF LIGHT

AMIN MAALOUF

The First Century
After Beatrice

Translated by Dorothy S. Blair

An *Abacus* Book

First published in Great Britain by Quartet Books Limited 1993
This edition published by Abacus 1994
Reprinted 1995 (twice), 1998, 2000, 2002, 2003
Published originally in French by Editions Bernard Grasset

Copyright © Editions Grasset & Fasquelle 1992
Translation copyright © Dorothy S. Blair 1993

The moral right of the author has been asserted.

A CIP catalogue record for this book is
available from the British Library.

ISBN 0 349 10599 5

Printed in England by Clays Ltd, St Ives plc

Abacus
An imprint of
Time Warner Books UK
Brettenham House
Lancaster Place
London WC2E 7EN

www.TimeWarnerBooks.co.uk

You are in the garden of an inn on the outskirts of Prague
You feel very happy a rose is on the table
And instead of writing your story in prose
You gaze at the beetle in the heart of the rose

Apollinaire, Alcools

To my mother

A

I was only one among many other witnesses of the events which I am consigning to these pages; I was closer to them than the horde of onlookers, but just as powerless. My name, I know, has been mentioned in books; this was formerly a source of some pride to me. No longer. The fly in La Fontaine's fable, *The Coach and the Fly*, could rejoice because the coach did arrive safely; what would it have boasted of if the journey had ended in a precipice? Such was in fact the part I played: that of a wretched insect flitting ineffectively around. At least I was never either dupe nor accomplice.

I have never been one to look for adventures, but sometimes adventure has sought me out. If I had been able to choose, I would have confined my adventures to the only world in which I have been passionately interested since my childhood and which, having duly celebrated my eighty-third birthday, I still find endlessly exciting: the world of insects, these remarkable Lilliputians – elegance, skill, age-old wisdom in miniature.

When talking to a lay public, I am in the habit of making it clear that I am by no means a defender of insects. In the case of the so-called superior animals, which we humans early enslaved and massacred in vast numbers, and over which we have triumphed once and for all, we can now allow ourselves to be magnanimous. Not in the case of insects. Between them and us, the daily, pitiless struggle continues, and nothing gives us reason to predict that man will be the victor. Insects were on this Earth long before us, they will still be here long after us, and when we are able to explore distant planets, we shall find their like rather than our own. Which, I think, will be a source of consolation to us.

As I said, I am not a defender of insects. But I am certainly one of their most ardent admirers. How could this not be the case? What creature has ever distilled materials nobler than silk, honey or the manna of Sinaï? Since time immemorial, man has striven to copy the texture and the taste of these products from insects. And what can we say, too, of the flight of the 'common' housefly? How many centuries shall we still need to be able to imitate it? Not to mention the metamorphosis of a 'humble' larva.

I could go on listing examples *ad infinitum*. This is not the purpose. In the following pages, it will not be a question of my passion for insects, but simply of the only moments in my life when I interested myself first and foremost in humans.

To listen to me, you could easily take me for a misanthropic bear. That would be far from true. My students' memories of me have been most favourable; my colleagues have had few bad words to say about me; I have at times been hospitable, but never excessively so; I have even cultivated, like a fallow field, two or three friendships. In particular, there was Clarence, and then Beatrice; but of them more later.

Let us say, to sum up honestly, that I have always found it hard to put up with the petty irritations of day-to-day misfortunes, but I have constantly lent a fresh ear to the great debates of our times.

Right up to the end of the century of my youth, I continued

to share its naïve enthusiasms, its naïve fears at the approach of the millennium: the recurring fears about the atom, then again of the Epidemic, and then of those holes in the ozone layer above the Poles – so many swords of Damocles. It was a great century, to my mind the greatest of all, perhaps the last great one, it was the century of all the crises and all the problems; today, in the century of my old age, the talk is only of solutions. I have always thought that Heaven invented the problems and Hell the solutions. Problems jostle us, knock us about, make us lose our complacency, take us out of ourselves. It is healthy to be thus thrown off our balance; it is through problems that all species evolve; it is solutions that cause them to stagnate and become extinct. Is it mere chance that the worst crime in living memory was called a 'solution' – the 'final solution'?

And everything that I observe all around me now, this stunted, morose, darkened planet, these waves of hatred, this universal chill enveloping everything, like a new ice age . . . is this not the fruit of a brilliant 'solution'?

Yet the end of the millennium had been magnificent, with a grand, infectious, devastating, messianic exhilaration. We all thought that, by degrees, the whole Earth was about to be touched by Grace, that all nations would soon be able to live in peace, freedom, abundance. From now on, History would no longer be written by generals, ideologues, despots, but by astro-physicists and biologists. Surfeited humanity would have no other heroes than inventors and entertainers.

I myself long cherished this hope. Like all of my generation, I would have shrugged my shoulders if anyone had predicted that so much moral and technical progress would prove to be irreversible, that so many avenues of exchange would be closed, that so many walls would rise up again, and all because of an omnipresent and yet unsuspected evil.

Through what odious trick of fate has our dream been destroyed? How did we reach this pass? Why was I forced to flee from the city and all civilian life? What I would like to relate here, as faithfully, as scrupulously as possible, is the slow emergence of the calamity which has been enveloping us from the first years of the new century, dragging us down into this decline, unprecedented, it seems to me, in its extent as well as in its nature.

In spite of the pervading terror, I shall try to write calmly to the end. At this moment I feel sheltered in my high mountain lair, and my hand scarcely trembles over the blank pages of this old indexed note-book, to which I am about to confide my scraps of truth. I even experience once more, as I recall certain images of the past, a feeling of lightheartedness which delights me so much that I momentarily forget the tragedy which I am supposed to relate. Is not one of the virtues of writing to be able to set down the trivial and the exceptional on the same flat sheet of paper? Nothing in a book seems any more profound than the ink in which it is written.

But an end to preambles! I had resolved to stick to the facts.

B

The whole thing began in Cairo, at a study-week in February, forty-four years ago. I even noted the day and time. But what's the use of juggling with dates, suffice to say that it was round about the year with three noughts. I have written 'began'? Began for me, I meant; historians place the beginning of the tragedy much further back in time. But I place myself here strictly from the point of view of a witness: in my eyes, the thing originated when I encountered it for the first time.

This introduction may lead you to think I belong to the race of great travellers: a date on the banks of the Nile, a jaunt to the Amazon or the Brahmaputra . . . Quite the contrary. I have spent most of my life at my desk, my travels have been, for the most part, between my garden and my laboratory. For which, moreover, I have not the least regret; every time I applied my eye to the microscope, this was like setting out on a voyage of discovery.

And when I really do happen to board a plane, it is also, nearly always, with the aim of observing an insect more closely. That trip to Egypt concerned the scarab beetle. But the viewpoint was not my usual one. Normally, when I took part in some symposium or other, it was merely a question of agriculture or epidemics. The guests of honour were the phylloxera or *propillia japonica*, the anopheles or tse-tse fly, for wearisome variations on a theme as old as prehistory: 'Our enemies from the animal kingdom'. The Cairo meeting promised to be different. The letter of invitation mentioned, and I quote, '. . . studying the place of the scarab in the civilization of Ancient Egypt: art, religion, mythology, legend.'

It will not be news to anyone, I presume, if I remind them that in the Pharaonic age the scarab was worshipped as a god. In particular, the species known in fact as 'the sacred scarab', *scarabeus sacer*, but in general all varieties of this noble insect. It was believed to be endowed with magical properties, and to be the depositary of the great mysteries of life. All through my years of study, every professor had repeated this to me in his own way, and as soon as I had my own laboratory in the Museum of Natural History, my students were also treated annually to my impassioned little eulogy of the scarab. Can one imagine what it means to anyone specializing in coleoptera to know that Ramses II would have bowed down before one of these little dung-eating creatures? The cult of the scarab even spread far beyond the borders of Egypt, to Greece, Phoenicia, Mesopotamia; Roman legionaries adopted the habit of engraving the outline of a scarab on the hilt of their swords; and the Etruscans carved its effigy on delicate amethyst jewels.

For my branch of study, I repeat, the scarab beetle is a celebrity, an aristocrat. I was about to say, a venerable ancestor. And, quite naturally, I have done some reading, some research into it; I couldn't mention it in the same breath as the common cockroach, all insects are not born on the same dunghill.

Yet, deep as my investigations had been, I felt immediately out of place at the Cairo symposium. Among the twenty-five participants from eight countries, I was the only one unable to read hieroglyphics, unable to name all the Tutmes or Amenophes; what is more, I alone knew nothing of Sacidic Copt and Subakhmimic Copt – please, don't ask me what this might be, I've never come across the word since, but I think I've transcribed it correctly.

As if everyone was in league to humiliate me, the speakers had all peppered their papers with apparently amusing Pharaonic expressions, which nobody obviously thought to translate, that's not done in their circles, it would be impolite to cast doubt in this way on the audience's erudition.

When it was my turn, I managed to say, only half joking, that, without being either an Egyptologist or archaeologist, and without knowing any Coptic dialect, I was not exactly an ignoramus, seeing that my speciality covered the three hundred and sixty thousand species of coleoptera that had already been identified, a third of all animate creatures – I do apologize for the small number! I also apologize for this sudden outburst of bragging, it's not my normal custom, but that day it was a vital necessity, to stop myself feeling choked by my own illiteracy!

Having made that point, and having discreetly confirmed its effect by my audience's expressions, I was then able to tackle my subject, namely a description of the feeding and reproductive habits of the scarab, to help us understand what, in its behaviour, could have appeared so suggestive, so mysterious, so richly instructive to the Pharaohs and their subjects.

I scarcely need to emphasize the fact that the ancient Egyptians, even four thousand years before us, were not a primitive people. They had already built the Great Pyramid, and if they gazed in amazement at an insect busy kneading buffalo dung, we should look on their wonder with respect.

What was the scarab beetle doing? Or rather, what does it do? Since the cult, of which it is the object, has not modified its behaviour.

With its forelegs it cuts a piece of dung which it rolls in front of it, to compress and round it. It has previously dug a hole in the sand, and when it has finished forming its little ball, it pushes it into the hole. Or even, first marvel, rather than taking it directly to the hole, it pushes it in the opposite direction, up to the top of a little mound of sand and there it lets go of it so that it rolls directly into the hole.

We think of Sisyphus; and, in fact, one of the best known varieties of scarab is called *sisyphus*. But the Egyptians saw in this another myth, another allegory. For, once the scarab has settled its little ball firmly in the hole, it gives it a pear shape so that it will not budge, then, in the narrow end it lays an egg from which a larva will emerge. At its birth it will find food in the little ball of dung and will continue to live there, in economic self-sufficiency, until its maturity. That is, until the new scarab leaves its 'shell' to repeat the same actions . . .

This rolling ball, said the Egyptians, symbolizes the movement of the sun in the firmament. And these scarabs which break out of their dung coffins symbolize resurrection after death. Are not the pyramids gigantic, stylized pear-shaped heaps of dung? Did they not hope that the deceased, like the scarab, would emerge one day, completely revived, to resume his labours?

If my paper left the audience somewhat unsatisfied, the one which followed, the work of a brilliant Danish Egyptologist, Professor Christensen, supported and enhanced it.

After politely thanking me for the zoological details which I had supplied, he expanded on the symbolical aspect. Starting from the presumed role of the scarab as messenger of resurrection, so he explained, all kinds of virtues had been attributed to it, in established religion as well as in popular beliefs. It had been set up as a symbol of immortality, thus of vitality, health and fertility. Stone scarabs used to be placed in sarcophagi, as well as scarabs made of hardened clay, which were used as seals.

'A seal,' noted the speaker, 'is affixed to the bottom of a document to certify its origin and guarantee its inviolability and perpetuity. Scarabs, symbols of eternity, were obvious choices for this use. And if the Pharaohs could return to life, they would observe that their precious archives, collected for thousands of years on papyrus, have all turned to dust, but the seals of hardened clay have survived. In its fashion, the sacred insect has kept its promise of immortality.'

Thousands of these scarab-stamps had been found, from which Egyptologists gleaned an abundance of information. The Dane, who seemed to have scrutinized every object in every museum in the world, from Chicago to Tashkent, had listed for us all the signatures – of Pharaohs, treasurers or priests of Osirus – as well as the wording of wishes which accompanied them. One of them appeared constantly like an incantation: 'May your name live for ever and a son be born to you!'

In order to amuse his audience, who might eventually have been bored by this repetition, Christensen suddenly took out of his pocket a little cardboard box which he held between his thumb and first finger and waved in front of our eyes. Coming at the end of a paper in which it was constantly a question of gold, emerald, carvings and incrustations, this recently and crudely made object was somewhat disturbing. This was exactly the effect desired by the speaker.

'I bought this yesterday evening in the Cairo main square, at Maydan al-Tahrir. Look at these flat capsules, shaped like beans, which in fact are called "Scarab beans". They contain a powder and the accompanying instructions say that if a man swallows this powder, his virility will be improved and, what is more, his ardour will be rewarded by the birth of a son.

As he spoke, the Egyptologist broke open one of the beans and emptied the powder on to the pages of his talk.

'As you see, the scarab is credited, in the eyes of some of our contemporaries, with some of the same magical properties as formerly. Moreover, the manufacturer is not an ignoramus, since there is here a very good reproduction of the scarab, as well as the translation, in Arabic and English, of the ancestral formula, which you know by heart: "May your name live for ever and a son be born to you!" '

There was a universal burst of laughter which Christensen silenced, like an experienced comedian with a raised eyebrow and an authoritative finger, as if he were preparing to make a major scientific communication.

'I must inform you that the said beans cost me a hundred dollars. I don't think that is the normal price, but I had taken the note out of my wallet and the urchin who was selling these objects snatched it out of my hands with an angelic smile before taking to his heels. That's an expense which the accountant at the University of Aarrhus will never reimburse me for!'

That same evening I made my way to Maydan al-Tahrir,

determined not to return without having acquired my own sample of 'scarab-beans' as a souvenir, and equally determined not to let myself be ripped off. As I left my hotel room, I was careful to take a ten-dollar note out of my wallet and put it in my pocket before carefully buttoning up my jacket.

Thus prepared, I could go off to brave the main square, a huge area not devoid of life, a maze of overhead walk-ways, supposed to reduce the swarming mass of humanity, but which on the contrary increased it by the addition of a third dimension. In this gigantic pushing and shoving throng of idle soldiers and bustling venders, in this jungle of gawking onlookers, thieves, beggars, traffickers of all sorts, I looked for my capsule-seller, or rather I tried to adopt a stupid, ecstatic expression, to make myself look as much like a tourist as possible, so as to lure him to me.

After a few short minutes I was spotted by two young venders. The smaller one automatically placed a box in my hand, I waved my ten-dollar note, determined to feign sincere annoyance if he demanded more. To my surprise he plunged his hand into his pocket to give me change. I indicated that he could keep the rest but he insisted on giving me what was owing, down to the last 'millime'. Why should I discourage such laudable intentions? So I resigned myself to waiting, amidst a deafening throng, till he had with difficulty collected in the palm of his hand the amount he had to give me back. They were only very insignificant coins, but it's the gesture which counts, isn't it? I thanked him with a pat on his shoulder and returned to the hotel looking for my Danish friend.

I found him in the bar, seated in front of one of his native beers. I proudly showed him my acquisition, informing him of the exact price I had paid. He congratulated me on my skill, joking about his complete naïvety when travelling, and when he was about to pay for the drinks I begged him, condescendingly, to leave it to me.

'You've paid enough for today.'

I unbuttoned by jacket. Nothing. My wallet had disappeared.

I would no doubt have omitted to relate this stupid and inglorious episode had it not weighed heavily on the resultant events.

In fact, when Christensen had spoken about these capsules, it had so amused me that I had resolved, as soon as I was back in Paris, to tell the story to my students and colleagues. A typically academic joke, you will say. I agree, but that is not the point: in a few hours, the 'scarab-beans' would have gone the rounds of the Museum, and among all those who laughed there would have been at least one to look more closely into the matter. Perhaps that would have allowed the mystery to be cleared up in time, and to avert the tragedy . . .

Instead of which, the moment I got home I couldn't wait to chuck the damned things into a drawer with a jumble of rubbish, never wanting to set eyes again on this material proof of my stupidity.

Ten days later I had forgotten all about it. Money earned or lost had never caused me lasting joy or annoyance. But at the time I had been furious. I had intended to buy some books from an antique bookshop in Qasr al-Nil Street that had been recommended to me; I had also spotted in the foyer of the hotel a beautiful reproduction of an antique-style scarab on papyrus, which I would have framed on my return. Deprived of any means of making payment, I had to give up the idea of these acquisitions, and on the last day of the trip, which had been left free, I was forced to stay in my room, reading and re-reading the conference papers.

So, the 'scarab-beans' remained in that drawer. And, as far as my brain was concerned, in a dark dungeon. They were only to emerge, alas, much later.

Meanwhile, there was the arrival – I almost said, the Advent – of Clarence.

C

It was a Monday, the first Monday since my return from Cairo, nevertheless I had already resumed all my habits and mislaid all my souvenirs. And when Professor Hubert Favre-Ponti came for his weekly visit, wearing his white lab. coat and carrying a paper cup of steaming coffee in each hand, there was no talk of scarabs or Egyptologists, but of journalists and migratory locusts.

Locusts, because my colleague had made a speciality of this scourge; journalists, because every time a country was devastated – generally in Sahelian Africa, and on an average one autumn in three – it was Favre-Ponti they came to interview. In this he seemed unduly privileged in the eyes of many colleagues who had chosen, like me, to study objects less harmful to humanity, and who were condemned thereby to pursue the most brilliant careers in the deepest obscurity.

If he was conscious of his luck, and the jealousy he inspired, Favre-Ponti never showed it. When 'his' plague made its appearance, he spent half his time receiving the press, the other half complaining about it.

'You know, my dear colleague, you see before you a youngster the same age as your students, and as soon as you launch into a thorough explanation, he stops taking notes, he stares at the ceiling and the bookshelves, or else he interrupts you in mid syllable and goes on to something else. What is more, you never know what nonsense he'll attribute to you the following day. Where you said, "Acrididae in gregarious phase", he misquotes you as saying, "a swarm of locusts".'

Perhaps Favre-Ponti was only trying to minimize his privilege to deflect his colleagues' thunderbolts. But that morning I only detected in his words an irritating and rather indecent self-satisfaction. Without ceasing to be polite, I wanted to put him in his place.

'I haven't often spoken to the press myself, but that's simply because I've never been asked. On the rare occasions that anyone's been kind enough to show an interest to me, I've been eager to reply. A little, to flatter my vanity, just like anyone else. But that wasn't the only reason. I've always thought it would be good for my mental health to address a non-captive audience as often as possible, people who don't expect me to give them a mark at the end of the year. That's the way to cure yourself of verbal mannerisms and give your jargon a good clean up. It wouldn't worry me in the least to say "locusts" instead of "Acrididae". I wouldn't say it to students of entomology. But to the general public, why not?'

'So, you'd be prepared to say "a swarm of locusts, fixing their greedy covetous eyes on green fields?" Well, go ahead, say it! There's a journalist coming to see me at eleven o'clock, I'll send her to you. Yes, yes, I'll send her to you.'

'You're not serious, Hubert, you know I'm not a specialist.'

'Do you think she'll notice the slightest difference?'

I'm not sure if these words, or the grimace which accompanied them, were intended to be at all complimentary to me. Moreover my colleague hastily dropped his empty cup into my waste-paper basket with a gesture of disdain, and left my office, roaring with laughter.

I didn't try to stop him. He had thrown out a challenge, pretending to be amused by it; it amused me also to take up the challenge.

Thus Clarence entered my life, at three minutes past eleven, with the compliments of Professor Favre-Ponti, 'unfortunately detained'. For the rest of my life, I was going to have this non-captive audience, this non-indulgent audience that I had wished on myself. Non-indulgent, but never disparaging. And, above all, untiring.

I feel obliged, at this stage, to introduce the word 'love', although it is no more scientific than 'locusts' . . .

Up till then I had only met one other person called Clarence, and that was a man, a very learned, very old Scottish entomologist; my Clarence was not so learned, nor so old. And so very much a woman.

I remember first letting my eyes rest on her lips, shells of deep magenta, pointing into the distance as in certain Egyptian frescos. Then gazing long at her shoulders. I always linger over shoulders, on them depends the elegance of the arms, neck, bust, skin; they determine one's bearing, the way one walks, the carriage of the head, the total harmony of movements, form; in a word, beauty. My visitor wore a white angora jumper, light but woolly, which drooped over her upper arms, leaving her superb, smooth, brown shoulders bare. A discreet offering, shoulders gracefully uncovered often inspire in me an ardent affection, a desire to caress them endlessly, and a wish to embrace.

In spite of all I have just written, I shall be close to the truth when I state that Clarence's beauty had little influence on our subsequent relationship. Not that I am, or ever have been, devoid of aesthetic sense, God forbid! But the only thing that can permanently attract me is the intelligence of the heart, providential if it is clothed in beauty, moving if it is not.

When 'the journalist' turned up, the only thing worrying me was my wager with Fabre-Ponti. So I had employed the minutes before the interview to prepare mentally what I was going to say, in what order, and in what words. I had to be, at one and the same time, clear to the general public and able to withstand the close examination of my peers; I knew no slip of the tongue would be condoned.

Clarence sat down facing me, with her knees tight together, like the most timid of my women students. But for me she was the examiner. And when, like the youngsters who so irritated my colleague, she suddenly stopped taking notes, I was really thrown. I stumbled over my words. I finished off my flights of eloquence in a couple of short sentences, and stammered, '. . . but perhaps I'm losing sight of what interests your readers?'

'Not at all, I assure you.'

I leaned over my desk, staring blatantly at her notebook.

'If there's a word you don't catch, don't hesitate to ask me to repeat it. You know, jargon is not easily got rid of.'

'I understand perfectly everything you say, please don't stop!'

Her smile was so dazzling and her protestation of sincerity so poignant. Only her 'Please don't stop!' did not mean, 'Continue your explanation, it interests me,' but rather, 'Don't switch off the music, it lulls me.' She confessed to me later that she had found me 'decorative and melodious'; at the time, she would not have dared utter such inappropriate epithets, but it was as if she had. I was not in the habit of being stared at like that, I had the intolerable feeling of being at the wrong end of the microscope.

'I'm not sure,' I said eventually, 'that this is the right sort of explanation for your readers.'

'Your explanations suit me perfectly. Only I was thinking of something else.'

'Your young mind was wandering elsewhere,' I announced most paternally.

'Not at all, my mind is wandering right here. Everything I see around me impresses me and makes me dream: this laboratory, this garden, the plants, insects, your white lab. coat, your old-fashioned spectacles, and especially this impressive desk with its drawers that contain so much mysterious, dusty knowledge, which will be a closed book to me all my life.'

She took a deep breath and shook her dark brown hair as if the better to wake herself up.

'There! I've told you what was distracting me. For you, everything around you must seem insignificant, without charm or poetry.'

'I must confess, this place no longer impresses me. And as for this desk, I must tell you it rather worries me. You see its impressive, massive looks but beneath this deceptive appearance, it is undermined by a network of galleries where colonies of wood-borers cavort gaily. Sometimes, in the evening, when I'm working late, I seem to hear the sound of their mandibles. And one day they will have worked so hard that I shall only have to put my briefcase down on this spot for everything to crumble, for this massive, respectable desk to fall to pieces, reduced to a heap of fly-speckled sawdust.

Perhaps only then will the administration think of providing me with a new one. Unless this whole decrepit building collapses at the same time.'

My visitor burst out laughing, she looked at me in the way any man would like to be looked at by a woman. Exhilarated, excited, reassured by seeing her replace the cap on her pen and put it away, I started on an unrestrained discourse about the Museum, lecturers, students, the Director – a gigantic, exuberant, caricatural fresco which would have delighted a reunion of alumni. But in the presence of a journalist I was seeing for the first time . . .

'You're not going to publish that!'

Only a forced smile gave, in the last extremity, some dignity to my anguished cry. Clarence gazed at me in silence. Never was an insect's soul examined so closely. It is true I regretted my chatter, I knew that every word she reported would cut me off irreparably from my students, my colleagues, this whole world in which I had chosen to lodge my useful existence. But that was not the question, not yet. Later, in a minute, in an hour, I would give way to remorse. Later, I would be ashamed. At that moment, there was this woman's gaze, I could not have borne to see that gleam of respect disappear, I would not have wanted for anything in the world to lower myself by any petty, trembling supplication.

'And now,' I said, stretching myself, 'now that I have entrusted you with my last will and testament, I can die in peace.'

By her laugh I knew that I had won.

It was more than I had any right to expect. Her article, which appeared ten days later, was a veritable love song to the Museum and its garden, 'An unappreciated oasis in the heart of an urban desert', 'ultimate refuge of deer . . . and old-fashioned scientists – in frock-coats, or nearly'. The specimen of such old-fashioned scientists was none other than myself, discreetly called 'Professor G.', and whom she described in affectionate terms with his 'long, lanky figure, terminating in the quiff on the top of his head and stooping so much that he would topple over if his heavy boots did not form a counterweight.' By means of her lyrical prose, she not only gave a picture of me as a researcher and teacher, she also gave the impression that I inspected the Zoological Garden and the animals every day; for two pins I'd be feeding the deer with my own hands. She no doubt needed this image of a rustic genius to justify her title 'In the Paradise of Professor G.' In brief, a mixture of truth and dream, from which I emerged, I have to say, immeasurably aggrandized.

Naturally, not a word of my confidences. But not the slightest allusion, either, to my laborious discourse on migratory locusts!

D

All this time, the box I had brought back from Cairo lay in my drawer beside a dismembered pair of nut-crackers; it was a Sunday when Clarence unearthed it, a Sunday which was important in my life, but for a reason which had nothing to do with this discovery. During all the months that we had been together, I had argued with her till I was blue in the face, trying to persuade her to come and live with me in the large flat I occupied at that time, in the rue Geoffroy-Saint-Hilaire, opposite the Botanical Gardens. And that Sunday, she had arrived.

I had phoned her as soon as her article appeared, we had met, chatted, whispered, embraced, clung to each other, made love unhurriedly but without wasting time, as if we had fixed this date since the dawn of civilization. We were both in love, delighted, incredulous, suddenly mischievous adults trespassing in a children's paradise. I know, from having observed all species, that love is merely a ruse for survival; but it is sweet to shut your eyes to this.

Everything in this affair seemed miraculous to me, all-embracing, and instantly definitive. It was probably so for Clarence too, but with the proviso that she did not wish to make a standing leap into a stranger's garden.

Perhaps I was wrong to show her my collection of coleoptera at our second meeting. I had at that time nearly three hundred specimens, including a magnificent Hercules Dynastid, my pride; apart from this collection, I also had a very rare scolopendra of exceptional size and a dwarf tarantula. By Clarence's initial reaction, I realized it would take some time to persuade her to 'cohabit with that lot', and that I ought to have prepared the way for this encounter with a little more tact. It was useless for me to repeat that these unfortunate defunct creatures were as inoffensive as a collection of old coins, that they were quite as valuable in my eyes and had the advantage of not being a temptation to burglars. Without attempting to contradict me, she made me promise, with ridiculous solemnity, that, from then on, any connection we as a couple might have with the world of insects should be exclusively, permanently, my responsibility.

It needed months of affection and guile on my part for her to overcome this unreasonable phobia and consent to set foot in my abode.

One foot only, she insisted. But I was no longer worried, I had lured her into becoming involved in the mechanics of a life together and every day I instinctively reinvented the thousand words and deeds that might tempt her to stay.

So Clarence had come to take possession of one corner of a wardrobe, two shelves in the bathroom and a drawer for her underclothes.

The said drawer being in this case the repository for a collection of every type of useless article: anything mouldy, rusty, broken, out-of-date . . . my companion had received orders to consign the lot to the dustbin, but she thought she ought first to check the labels on my medicines.

'No date on this one, it must last for ever.'

I looked at the box which she was showing me.

'You don't know how right you are, it's a recipe from the time of the Pharaohs.'

I told her about it. Cairo, the symposium on the scarab . . . and even the young rascals in the Maydan al-Tahrir.

She listened, all ears. Then she tipped the contents into her lap and began to read the instructions.

'I've heard of these strange beans before, but this is the first time I've seen any. Last summer a Moroccan friend offered to bring me some back; I was ashamed to show any interest. I expected some witch's brew, but this is nicely packaged.'

She read on.

'Are you sure you didn't buy this so you could have a son and heir?'

There was a feline mistrust of the male species in her eyes. I raised my right hand in a pitiable oath which Clarence accepted with a laugh. I took advantage of this to go over to the attack.

'The Danish Egyptologist explained to me that men often hesitate to swallow these beans, so their women-folk open the capsules and sprinkle the powder in their soup, without their knowing.'

'Yes, I know, misogyny is handed down in the first place from mother to daughter. When you've grown up as I did on the shores of the Mediterranean, you don't have much chance of forgetting this.'

Her family, originally from Bessarabia, had lived in Salonika, Alexandria, Tangiers, then Sète, where Clarence was born. Her surname has been distorted, shortened, lengthened many times before becoming Nesmiglou. Could I resist occasionally calling my companion 'igloo' when we were alone? Teasing her mischievously I explained one day that this nickname suited her perfectly. 'What is an igloo? A block of ice, in the shelter of which one feels warm . . .'

Apart from her name, Clarence retained from the century-old nomadic existence of her family the best aspects of cross-breeding: a decidedly sunburnt Greek Venus, with an accent from Provence, who I always visualized lying on some beach, naked and wet with spray, gazing into the distance.

That Sunday, she stood up, still clutching the box of beans, and began to pace slowly up and down the room, her face tilted with a drawn expression. On so many occasions I would gaze at her lovingly as she walked to and fro, wanting to stop her and throw my arms around her, but I would never try to do so, not once would I intrude on her pacing or her thoughts, merely would I watch and wait, for I knew an idea was simmering and would always emerge, whether serious or frivolous, sometimes both at once, and she would eventually tell me about it.

'Don't you think this would be a good idea for my "maggot"?'

The scarab beans, good for Clarence's maggot?

'It's our newspaper jargon,' she said with a laugh. 'The senior staff take turns to write a humorous column which is boxed, with their by-line and photograph. This week, for the first time, I'm entitled to write my "maggot". I've been fighting for this, and ever since the editorial committee gave their permission, I've been trying in vain to find an idea that's out of the ordinary. And here it is.'

She was holding the box carefully, as if it were an exhibit in a court case. And she resumed her pacing up and down our bedroom, like an impatient predator. For a long time. Before coming to an abrupt stop.

'My article's done, I've only got to write it down,' she exclaimed triumphantly.

Then she sank exhausted, dog-tired, on to the bed, holding her arms out-stretched.

I could now intrude.

'Clarence Nesmigloo's Maggot' consisted of a few seamlessly constructed paragraphs around a simple idea, spiralling on to stop dead at its logical punch-line.

I no longer have the text to hand, but a summary in my prosaic language would go more or less as follows: 'If tomorrow, men and women could, by some simple means, determine the sex of their children, certain peoples would only choose boys. Thus they would cease to breed and would in time disappear. The cult of the male, that today is simply a defect in society, would become collective suicide. In view of the rapid progress of science, with which people's mentalities have not kept pace, such a hypothesis will not fail to be confirmed in the near future. If we can believe the Cairo scarab, this is already the case.'

If I had wished, I could have reproduced Clarence's exact words, so much more elegant than mine. I deliberately refrained from doing so. The whole thing was expressed in a tone that was both angry and light-hearted which, re-read today, after everything that has happened, would appear monstrous.

Monstrous? How little is this word like Clarence! There was possibly some frivolity on her part, but that is the rule of the genre; a 'maggot', a humorous column, is a butterfly, it has to be airy and frivolous. There was also a certain casualness, but is not this our common lot? We know this now, the media is responsible for a casual attitude as surely as light is responsible for shadow; the stronger the projector, the denser the shadow. The newspapers had certainly reported some curious phenomena from time to time. In China, for example, it had been noted that, starting in the eighties, more boys than girls were born in certain provinces; specialists had then calmly explained that families, forced by the authorities to have no more than one child, were getting rid of the first born, if it had the bad taste to turn up without the indispensable appendage; thus there would have been several million infanticides. The world commiserated for forty-eight hours. Then the whole matter had fallen into the universal mill and ground into an everyday occurrence.

I'm not trying to excuse Clarence, I know she was wrong to joke about the 'auto-genocide of misogynous peoples', but we have to put ourselves into the minds of people at the time, when you had to be instantly affected by everything and never to worry for long about anything. 'Such and such an African metropolis is about to be decimated by Aids' was screamed out one day. Was it true? false? exaggerated? imminent? hypothetical? Everything was deafened by the same surrounding din. And, in spite of the salutary company of my insects, I myself was deafened for too long.

This is by way of explanation why no one has the right to cast the first stone at Clarence. She wrote ironically, her readers were amused. The only letter she received after the publication of her article was from a lady who asked her for precise information about the 'scarab-beans' and where they could be procured.

For my part, the subject dealt with by my companion

provided me with the ideal excuse to tackle a subject which was much on my mind: was this not the moment, for her and for me, to have a child? I was forty-one, she was twenty-nine, we were not pressed for time, physiologically I mean; but it was useful to think about it. Clarence did not disagree with the principle of a child, still less about having a child by me. But she said, rightly, she was 'doing well' on her paper, she was anxious to write and be read, she was anxious and impatient to travel all over the world. Were there not wonders under every sky waiting to be described, scandalous abuses waiting to be denounced? She planned investigations in Russia, Brazil, Africa, New Guinea . . . To become pregnant in the immediate future would have been, in her words, 'like shooting herself in the foot'; and so would a very young child. Later, she promised, when she was better known and virtually irreplacable, she could take a year off. For our child.

I had to agree to this arrangement, intending to return to the attack as soon as I felt the moment was opportune. I couldn't rush Clarence, but I had to take my own impatience into account.

I don't know if many men resemble me in this, but I always wanted, even as an adolescent, to hold a little girl of my own flesh and blood in my arms. I always thought that would be a kind of fulfilment, without which my life as a man would remain incomplete. I constantly dreamed of a daughter, whose features and voice I imagined, and I had named her Beatrice. Why Beatrice? There must have been a reason, but as far back as I can remember, I can discover no source for this name, it is simply there, like the unfolding frond of a fern.

When I uttered this name for the first time in Clarence's

presence, she said she was jealous, and laughed out loud to make me think she was joking. But her laughter did not ring true. She had just realized that I could not go on loving her if she made me give up this dream. And that she had to resign herself to cohabiting for ever in my little world with Beatrice, much more intimately than with my collection of coleoptera.

From now on, the two women were to be for me the object of the same loving worship. I was determined, as soon as Clarence took the promised year off, to apply for a sabbatical myself, for paternity leave.

Long before I knew the date, I had christened it 'the year of Beatrice'.

E

It was only after a long wait, many fights, and endless arguments that Clarence's paper decided to send her on her first important mission abroad, to India, in this case, to report on wives who were being burnt to death. Not only those whom a cruel tradition formerly condemned to be cremated beside their deceased husbands, but also often quite young brides, whose in-laws drenched them in paraffin out of sordid motives to do with legacies; a more recent custom and one which, alas! has not yet disappeared.

The investigation was to last ten days, with a final stop-over in Bombay, from where Clarence was to take a night flight, due to arrive in Paris at six o'clock on Friday morning.

The previous evening, however, just when I thought her about to leave, I heard her voice at the other end of a crackling, breathy line, asking me, after a hasty greeting, if I knew where the beans brought back from Cairo were.

Putting the receiver down, I took the box out of the drawer where it had remained, the sole survivor of the grand clear-out, and now surrounded by soft underwear, impregnated with Clarence's perfume.

'I need you to read me the instructions for use. In English.'

Just like that, on the line from Paris to Bombay?

'You sound very far away, Clarence,' I said by way of protest.

'Tonight, when you close your eyes, imagine you're near me and holding me tight. If you're alone, I mean.'

'I promise! If I'm alone.'

'And if you aren't alone, let me know, so I can stop stupidly acting the faithful wife!'

Two peals of knowing laughter, a long conspiratorial silence. Then she returned, without any transition, to her immediate concern.

'If you could speak loudly and as distinctly as possible. I'm going to record it so I can listen to it again at leisure.'

After she had made me repeat the most obscure words, she announced her decision to stay on a little longer, asking me to let her paper know.

This I hastened to do first thing the next morning. Muriel Vaast, her editor, seemed surprised and annoyed. Clarence had phoned her earlier to let her know she'd finished her investigation and that she had an article of six pages at least and some completely new photographs.

'. . . And just when we're ready to go to press, she phones to say she won't be back in time. That's not very professional, you must admit!'

'I suppose,' I muttered, like the parent of a naughty schoolchild, 'she must have got hold of some fresh, important details at the last minute.'

'I hope so, for her sake!'

I too hoped so, for her sake, and worried about the hostile reception awaiting her on her return. I had never met Muriel Vaast, I only knew her from the summary description Clarence had given me: 'She looks like a sort of fat foreman in crumpled skirts', and I have to say that this first telephonic contact didn't leave me with the impression of excessive human warmth. I knew my companion could expect from her neither goodwill nor indulgence. But if she brought back a scoop from Bombay she might manage perhaps to extort some respect from her.

I did not realize my error until Wednesday evening, when I saw tears in Clarence's eyes for the first time since we had been together.

She had arrived in Paris in the early afternoon, and taken a taxi straight to the paper, where an editorial committee was in session.

Exuberant, in spite of the fatigue of the journey, she had pushed the door open with a laugh, joined her hands to greet the assembly with a mock exotic bow, drawn a chair noisily up to the table and begun to unpack her papers . . . Only to hear this weary groan: 'All right, let's recap! You're in Bombay, with an article and photographs that we're waiting for in Paris, and for which, at your request, we held six whole pages. Suddenly, at the eleventh hour, you choose to upset your plans and ours. I suppose something extraordinary happened. What is it? I can't wait to hear.'

After this chilly welcome, Clarence no longer felt much inclined to justify herself. She took a long look at the editor, then at her colleagues, stared at the ceiling, at the door. Hesitated. Placed a hand on her papers, as if about to pick them up. Hesitated again . . . And then resigned herself to giving the required explanations. Wrongly, it seems to me, for, coming after such a prelude, anything she said would naturally seem futile, trivial, ridiculous. In any case, what she had to say revealed nothing spectacular or exceptional. However, anyone listening to her without prejudice, with a little imagination and just the teeniest bit of goodwill, would have glimpsed beneath my friend's hesitating words, the rough outlines of the approaching tragedy.

31

What did she say? To fill in the time before leaving Bombay, she had decided to take a walk along the Marine Drive towards Chowpatti where, caught up in the multi-coloured throng of pedestrians, she had bumped into a stall on hinged legs and knocked it over. On this stall a young lad had laid out piles of boxes for sale, which the passers-by were eagerly grabbing. Partly out of curiosity and partly also in the hope of excusing her clumsiness, she had bought one, only to discover that it was almost an exact replica of the one I had brought back from Cairo the previous year, except that a picture of a cobra was rolled round the one of the scarab. That was when she phoned me, to compare the instructions; they were almost identical, with a few minor adaptations.

Perhaps she might not have paid so much attention to this coincidence if, two days before, in the course of her investigation in a Gujarati village, she had not met an ancient crone, with skin like parchment, who had told her an astonishing story. After bewailing the fate of her grand-daughter who had been sacrificed a few weeks after her wedding, the old woman had predicted that this tragedy would never occur again in future, since in that village, and everywhere around, only boys were being born, as if girls, warned of the misfortune which awaited them, preferred not to come into the world.

On examining the boxes which bore the portentous inscription in large letters, FAMILY ENERGY MIRACLE, but which the vendor eloquently abbreviated to 'Boy Beans', Clarence immediately recalled the old woman whose voice had emerged in gasps from her toothless mouth, like that of the Delphic oracle. Intrigued, 'shocked for no good reason', as she admitted, and wishing to make further investigations to complement her original project, she had chosen to postpone her return and the next day had visited a large maternity hospital in Bombay, in the hope of meeting some gynaecologist there who might tell her, at the very least, if there were any grounds for her perplexity.

The building had been recently repainted and was situated in magnificent grounds, impeccably maintained, with not the slightest resemblance to the hospitals and clinics she had seen in the country up till then. At first they received her like a maharanee. But as soon as she uttered the word 'journalist', and before she even had time to say she had come to investigate the imbalance of male and female births, the smiles disappeared; suddenly no doctor could receive her, neither that day, nor on Monday, nor during the coming weeks. Only one person could spare a minute to chat to her: a male nurse with a large moustache whom she ran into near the entrance gate, just as she was leaving. He was quite prepared to tell her in confidence that, 'this nursing-home is certainly blessed by heaven, since nearly all the babies born here are boys'.

At this point in Clarence's story, the editorial committee was divided: one third was coughing discreetly and two thirds were shaking with laughter. 'We've got our lead article for page one,' declared one charitable colleague. 'Exclusive confidences of a Bombay nurse: "We see nothing but willies now!"'

'If I understand correctly,' commented the editor, frowning nevertheless at those who were laughing the most unrestrainedly, 'everything started with an observation: that the same capsules are sold in Cairo and in Bombay. I must tell you, for your information, that in Macao, Taipei and all other towns in South-East Asia, you can find hundreds of manufacturers of remedies, ointments, plasters, elixirs, all reputed to be miraculous, made from moonstones, gorillas' toenails, scarab shells, not forgetting rhinocerous horn, which are the object of sordid, lucrative, nauseating, traffickings. There have always been millions of ignoramuses who believe in this nonsense and make a fortune for the quacks; I hope, this is a temporary aberration, Clarence, as far as you're concerned. We count on you to deal with questions that interest women, and God knows there are enough of those, important, engrossing, heart-rending questions. But if you try to fob us off with old-wives'-tales, then we're no longer on the same wavelength.'

Clarence could have defended herself; she could have explained that they were completely wrong about where her interests lay . . . But what was the use of going on in such an atmosphere? She now had only one aim, and that was not to give way in public, now that her legs and shoulders were feeling the after-effects of the tiring journey. She managed to put a brave face on it, without any beseeching glance. But she said nothing more. In any case, she could no longer control her voice.

Did I write that she shed tears? It was that same night, in our bed, with my arms around her, as if to keep out the dazzle of the outside world. I was much more shaken than she was by her silent sobbing, and thought the best thing was for me to act the protective male and whisper in her ear, 'Have a good cry tonight, but tomorrow you'll begin to fight back. People can only be defeated by their own bitterness.'

Then I added, with a naïve solemnity, dictated by my extreme emotion, 'If need be, I will help you.'

She found the strength to smile again, raised herself on her elbows to place a tender kiss on my lips. And then dropped back immediately.

'Even if I spoke under the stress of emotion, you ought to take my offer seriously. I'm convinced that, in some respects, your job is not very different from mine.'

'Really, I'd like to know in what ways a journalist is like an entomologist. But look out! Watch what you say! I chose you just because you belong to a different world from mine. If you manage to prove the contrary, I'll leave you.'

This time she sat up in bed properly and my cheeks could confirm that her tears were beginning to dry.

'It is my firm conviction,' I deliberately exaggerated, 'that we are both doing more or less the same job. I spend part of my time observing insects, describing them, listing their names. But the most exciting thing in my subject is the study of metamorphosis. From the larva to the insect by way of the nymph.

'The word "larva" has acquired, in current language, a slimy association. However, according to its Greek origin, larva simply means mask. Because the larva is nothing but a disguise: one day, the insect leaves off its disguise to show its true image. And, as you no doubt know, the scientific name for the insect which has reached its definitive form is "imago".

'From the larva to the insect, from the ugly, crawling caterpillar to the magnificent butterfly with its true colours displayed, we have the impression of passing from one reality to another; and yet, everything which will form the beauty of the butterfly is there in the caterpillar. My job allows me to read the image of the butterfly or the scarab or the trap-door spider in the larva. I look at the present, and I perceive the image of the future, isn't that wonderful?

'And the journalist? Where does his passion lie? Is it solely in the observation of human butterflies, human spiders, their hunting and their love affairs? No. Your job becomes sublime, incomparable, when it allows you to read the image of the future in the present, for the entire future is to be found in the present, but masked, coded, in a dispersed order. Am I then not right to say that we are almost colleagues?'

If my argument did not succeed in convincing Clarence, it did at least have the merit of cheering her up.

After a few seconds she dozed off, with her face buried in the hollow of my shoulder, while I remained a prey to the best kind of insomnia, the sort when ideas jostle and tumble over each other, when the most obscure mysteries seem pierced with brief flashes of light, like a cave caught in a thunder storm.

I won't go so far as to claim that I understood everything that night. I would say, more modestly, at the risk of sounding confused, that, as I listened to my companion sleeping, inhaled her moist warm breath and gazed affection-ately at the last traces of tears on her cheeks, I suddenly understood that there was something to understand. Some-thing essential, probably.

So I decided to talk to somebody in whom I had long had the utmost confidence.

F

I don't remember Clarence ever meeting André Vallauris. He was my closest friend, but our friendship was not the kind that could put up with any intrusion, even from the women we loved.

Our friendship went back to before I was born, as he was already my father's friend and a sort of godfather to me. I say 'a sort of', because there was no question of a christening, but rather of sponsoring me through my life, a function he fulfilled with a singular mixture of warmth and solemnity.

We were in the habit of meeting twice a year, on the last Sunday in October, for my birthday which falls on the 31st, and the first Sunday in March, for his, as he was actually born on 29 February, that mischievous date of birth, shared by a few rare individuals. No need for us to phone, to ring back or confirm; no question of cancelling, or altering the time or place .... On the day in question, I would turn up at his home at four o'clock; he would see to it that he was alone in the large flat, with its cream panelled walls and endless corridors. I would follow him, to find the teapot already on the table and the aroma of bergamot already rising from our two steaming cups next to our twin armchairs.

As I sat down, I would place on the table, nearer his cup

than mine, a box of *pets-de-nonne*,* bought at his favourite confectioner's; he would undo the ribbon and invariably say, 'You shouldn't have!' But naturally, I did have to, it was our custom, it fuelled our conversation. Moreover, he couldn't resist them, except when there was only one left. Which he offered me. Which I refused. And which he snapped up, I'm sure, the moment I'd gone.

It will surprise no one if I add that André was a big man. The correct word would be 'obese'. Big, bearded and obese. In my eyes, and from my pen, this term is not automatically a reproach. There is obese and obese. André was one of those men who seem to have ballooned around an ordinary silhouette by a sort of harmonious expansion, and inside this casing, and possibly to belie it, developed a greater refinement of mind and senses than other people.

But I am a little ashamed now of having tried to describe André Vallauris by way of a digression about the *pets-de-nonne*, rather than through the presents which he gave me in return.

I remember, as a matter of fact, that at the end of my very first visit, he walked over to his bookcase at the other end of the sitting-room. All the volumes were in antique leather bindings and from a distance all looked alike. He took one down and gave it to me. *Gulliver's Travels*. I could keep it. I was nine years old, and I don't remember whether on my next visit I noticed that there was still a gap where the book had been. Only, over the course of the years, the bookcase was studded with similar gaps until it resembled a toothless mouth. Not once did we remark on this, but I eventually

---

* Very light little fritter-like cakes made from choux pastry. The name literally means 'nun's fart'.

realized that these places would remain empty; that for him they were now as sacred as the books; and that these phantom volumes, carved out of the buff-coloured leather, represented all men's unspoken love and the pride they took in plundering their own collections.

While my father was alive, I sometimes met André on other occasions, but then our relationship was no different from that of the other guests, nothing that could recall, even by allusion, 'our' conversation. This use of the singular noun was obligatory; often, from one season to another, André would greet me with an imperceptibly challenging 'Now, where were we?', or else by, 'As I was saying . . .' It was a game, everything with him was a game. But does not a game cease to be a game when it lasts all one's life and laughter never washes over it? I could count on him to maintain this stimulating ambiguity indefinitely.

What was our conversation about? Often about the books he had given me. Thus, on the subject of *Gulliver*, we had long discussions about the violent quarrel which divided the Lilliputians over the way to cut open their eggs, at the big end or the little end; we tried to enumerate the conflicts which, in the world we knew, could be compared to the quarrels between the Big-Endians and the Little-Endians. Inspired by the various books, our subjects were as different as *Don Quixote* is from *The Divine Comedy* or Aldous Huxley's *Brave New World*. But it was not only books; I had everything to discover, and André possessed the time-honoured art of great teachers – that of making you feel you have always had in you what they have just that moment taught you.

Recently, we had mainly talked about women and the times, that is the age of creatures and ideas. We also talked about my profession which intrigued him. And even more often about his.

As a child he had dreamed of becoming an inventor; his father wanted him to be a lawyer. He had obeyed. But had sneaked in by the back door, to return to his first love: he had in fact devoted himself to the law associated with the new technology, a branch which he had had a hand in setting up. From magnetic charts to *in vitro* fertilization, from radio-active fall-out to orbital stations, a thousand new facts of life had given rise to law-suits which no code of law had foreseen; 'piracy', 'plagiarism', 'property', 'nuisance' no longer had their customary meaning; and even words such as 'life' and 'death' had to be redefined. For André Vallauris, every case was a pretext for interminable investigations which often continued well after the end of the case, and which were not always over scientific or judicial questions; there were often, hidden in his files, much trickier questions of conscience, he claimed, than in the criminal proceedings.

He discussed all these aspects of his work with me, often sounding out my feelings and, I believe, giving them due consideration. It goes without saying that I, for my part, had the highest respect for his opinions. Nevertheless, when I put some problem to him that was bothering me, it was not always to ask for advice. I had another motive which, at the time, I would have been unable to detect, but which today seems obvious and clear: I think that throughout our friendship, I 'planted' ideas in André's mind, in the way one dumps a load, or drops a seed on familiar ground. In his head nothing was lost, everything progressed, and when I met my idea again it had grown roots and branches; often, too, it had been refined to the point where I no longer recognized it.

*

As luck would have it, my next meeting with my friend was on the Sunday following Clarence's return; I had already told him about our relationship; I informed him of our wish for a child. Then I expounded at greater length on her trip to India, her investigations, her problems with the paper, all in very great detail and with a certain amount of heat.

André listened to me with his usual attention. Remained thoughtful for a few moments which seemed long to me. Then asked, quite seriously, 'And if it were a boy, you haven't thought of another name besides Beatrice?'

It was, to be sure, the question I least expected. But it was part of our game never to show surprise about anything.

'No,' I replied in the same tone, 'I'm not anticipating any other name.'

He picked up his cup, sipped his tea. Before starting on a quite different topic. The parenthesis was closed.

At least, that's what I was naïve enough to think.

A month had gone by, and even a few days more, when I received a note in Vallauris's handwriting.

'I wanted to send you this.' 'This' was a page photocopied from an English encyclopaedia, with one paragraph circled in brown felt pen. It read, 'In the seventies, following an outbreak of measles in certain villages in Senegal, a sudden imbalance was noted in the birth-rate: only one girl was born for every ten boys; the same inexplicable phenomenon was observed subsequently in other parts of the world.'

I passed the letter to Clarence who was opening her mail beside me. It must have been nine o'clock, and we had been sitting for some time at the breakfast table in front of the bay window overlooking the Botanical Gardens. It was the most delightful time of the day for us, we would not have exchanged it for any future time.

'Read these few lines. This is possibly the explanation of what happened in the old lady's village in Gujarat.'

She took the letter and glanced through it.

'Perhaps.'

She would have said 'perhaps' in the same tone if, for example, I had expressed the opinion that the honey that morning was better than the one I usually bought. Yes, the same polite indifference. Except that she got up from her chair earlier than expected.

'I'll have my shower before you.'

As I watched her slip away I smiled. She made me think of a woman who had been reminded of a former love affair, which she didn't deny but had no wish to restart.

That was more or less how I interpreted the matter, and when André sent me a second letter, ten days later, I avoided mentioning it to Clarence. Moreover these missives were to become more and more frequent. I was not particularly surprised. If in fact Vallauris could go for years without writing to me or phoning, simply relying on our ritual twice-yearly meetings, there had been occasions however when, in reply to some problem I had put to him, he had bombarded me with similar photocopied pages, scarcely annotated. Having said that, on the rare occasions when he had done so, it had never been so enthusiastically. It was a deluge! I had already received ten letters in three months when I decided to show one to Clarence again.

It was a short item from the *Times of India*, reproduced in a London Sunday paper, reporting that a group of Indian doctors had denounced 'an odious practice which is spreading, which everyone knows about but which no one thinks of stopping . . . Thousands of pregnant women, informed too soon of the sex of the child they are bearing, ask for an abortion if it is a girl. Certain nursing homes even boast that all the babies they deliver are boys.'

This time she showed the interest I reckoned on. But her comment . . .

'So, I was wrong.'

'How, wrong?'

I could have grabbed her by the shoulders and shaken her!

'I was convinced the scarab beans were at the root of what I'd seen in India. It turns out that in Gujarat, it was probably a measles epidemic; and in the Bombay maternity home, it was illegal abortions.'

'Damn the scarab! My own impression, from everything I've read, is that you came back from that trip with a heap of information and hunches which your colleagues didn't take seriously, and which have all been confirmed. We are faced with some alarming phenomena which deserve serious investigation, in India as well as many other countries. Isn't this a thousand times more important than stories about beans?'

'We're not talking about the same thing. I'd have liked . . .'

Her voice trailed away, as if from exhaustion. I was about to take advantage of her silence to remonstrate further with her, when I caught the expression in her eyes and I stopped. She looked more serious – worse, more distressed – than I had ever seen her before. Taking her hand in mine, then lifting it gently to my lips, in my customary way, I was about to ask her, very tactfully, what was upsetting her so much, when she pulled herself together, and gave a faint smile, as if her only problem was to find suitable words.

'What I like about the scarab beans is that they let me

formally confound all the misogynists. But I wouldn't for the world be side-tracked into the endless argument over abortion.

'As soon as you utter certain words, you know, it's like squeezing a drop of lemon juice into a glass of warm milk. It immediately separates into curds and whey. If you say "abortion", people immediately begin to protest; their reflexes, their tropisms re-surface. No matter what subtle distinctions you make, they shut their ears, you must hurriedly choose which side of the barricade you're on. Some classify you with the "bigots", others with the "butchers". However, in my mind, the bigots are no better than the abortionists: didn't they invent original sin, according to which woman is the cause of all ills, and if it were not for her greed, her stupidity, the human race would still be living in the Garden of Eden? Didn't they invent the story that woman was born from man's rib and that God, who logically ought to be both father and mother of all creatures, was only their father?

'For thousands of years, people have never stopped praising the male, the whole of mankind has wanted to see only boys born. And today, a miracle! The wish can be fulfilled. Baby girls can now be thrown out with the bathwater. Who protests? The bigots. Whereas, some of the people who are for the equality of the sexes prefer to look the other way.

'And you'd like to see me get mixed up in this fools' debate!'

G

Having regard for Clarence's frame of mind since she got back from her trip, I took good care not to show her the rest of the material Vallauris sent me, all the more so since most of it referred to events going back to the beginning of the nineties. I myself only glanced at the articles before putting them away in a plastic folder, out of consideration for my friend André, and to satisfy my conscience.

But when the date of my ritual visit to him came round, I made it my duty to re-read the lot more attentively. I was a little ashamed of this schoolboy 'swotting', but my godfather was sometimes apt to cross-question me. He would be courteous, friendly, but relentless. Ever since my childhood, whenever he gave me a book, he presumed that before our next meeting I would have read it carefully. 'Read slowly,' he recommended, 'and without making notes, only too often one gets away with scribbling something illegible instead of planting it in here'; and he pressed his forefinger hard against his forehead. He would easily have noticed if I hadn't glanced at anything new since our last meeting. 'If, in twenty years, you've read, what I call seriously read, forty real books, then you'll be able to look the world in the face.'

So I read, 'what I call seriously read', that is re-read and chewed over his ten or so dispatches.

*

'I'd be curious to know what most held your attention out of all the material I sent you.'

These were the words with which André greeted me. So, as soon as we had taken our usual seats, I told him about my discussion with Clarence. Then I added more specifically, 'On the whole, I have the impression we've got a curious charade on our hands. I don't know if the syllables are in the right order, and I don't know if there's an answer at the end either.'

'If we'd met last Sunday, I'd have confessed to being just as puzzled. All I'd been doing was to pick things up here and there, following my instinct, playing by ear. But on Thursday, I woke up with a fixed idea, and I spent the day at the library, wading through columns of figures, through ratios which recurred on page after page, only varying by an infinitesimal fraction. I was about to give up when I caught sight of a display shelf showing a study on the population of ten large towns around the Mediterranean, including Cairo, Naples, Athens and Istambul. Here again were enough figures to make your head spin, but accompanied by long analyses. The authors set down in black and white that they have noted everywhere an appreciable increase in male births and a "significant" decline in female births. Normally, there are on an average one hundred and five boys born for every hundred girls; the figures for this enquiry give from one hundred and twelve to one hundred and nineteen boys per hundred girls, according to the towns. Nothing spectacular to a layman, but if the authors are to be believed, a discrepancy on such a large scale is unprecedented.

'Is it a question of a phenomenon similar to the one the Indian doctors denounced? I'm far from knowing the real story. At least, since Thursday, I'm aware that there is a riddle, and that other people besides me are puzzling their heads over it.'

I had never before gone away from André's with such a feeling of being left hanging in the air. Normally, as soon as I heard the door slowly close behind me, with the clunk a piece of machinery makes when it is obstructed, I would stroll off, sunk in thought, my feet scarcely seeming to touch the ground. It was not on account of all that I learnt from my godfather; I had other means of obtaining information. It was not so much his erudition that I envied as the ease with which he passed from one field to another, surveying the problems of the world with an eagle eye.

I hope no one will insult me by suggesting that I was taken in by his gift of the gab or by any lawyer's court-room tricks; that was not what made up the essence of our encounters. I would merely say, in all seriousness, that André's intelligence was proportionate to his weight; that is to say, he had that sort of massive conviction, expressed without false modesty, that everything in this world – laws, science, religion, states – has been made by men like himself, like me, and that everything could consequently be criticized, ridiculed, demolished, recons-tructed. 'We are not guests on this planet, it belongs to us as much as we belong to it, its past belongs to us, as does its future.'

Such confidence was not in my nature. I have always had an acute sense of my own insignificance, I too say this without false modesty or shame; when I looked at the world around me, it was not with the thought of overturning it; I am not a law-maker, scarcely more than an observer only too happy to discover some forgotten article in the laws of zoology; only too happy also, as one individual among

billions like me, to play the game of survival and reproduction, within the limits of my strength, and my allotted
span of life. In my subject one acquires an acute sense of the
ephemeral and one learns to be resigned to it.

My association with Vallauris was beneficial by virtue of
this different approach. He has ceaselessly provided me with
my dose of self-assurance. The day after our meeting, I
always set to work again with a fierce desire to succeed.

Not this time. I left, on the contrary, with the feeling of
running away. I had stayed as long as usual, till the
penultimate *pet-de-nonne*, three full hours, but in fact I had
simply played a walk-on part. In his own proud, lofty
manner, André had launched ten calls for assistance, sending
ten articles of which not one had aroused any real curiosity
on my part. On no point had I engaged in the slightest
research, nothing had elicited from me the slightest unexpected comment, and in the course of our meeting, I had
been content to watch my friend, gauge his tentative moves,
his indecision, whereas I had been the one to seek his advice. I
was well aware that he took pleasure in these investigations,
but on that afternoon, it was not just a matter of intellectual
excitement, there was a certain anxiety and sense of urgency
which accorded ill with the image I had of him.

My immediate explanation was ungenerous: his age.
André was seventy-one; he had long since given up court
appearances, but he had only recently given up his chambers.
I have often criticized my fellow-men for their propensity to
consider people in other age-groups as special cases, being
oneself, at every age, the general case, the permanent seat of
normality. I criticize, I get angry, I mock; but I have to
confess that I am not proof against this fault. On that day, I
was in the mood to be satisfied with such a hasty explanation.

Thus easily reassured, I decided nevertheless to devote more time in future to André's despatches. And to send him, myself, a few newspaper cuttings now and then.

If I had time. As I was then busy preparing a public lecture. It had been announced for 8 December, and it was already November and I had not written the first line.

Not out of lack of interest, on the contrary! Out of excess of enthusiasm. I had spent so much time in research that I had continually put off the moment of writing. The subject of my lecture – God knows how unreal it seems now, but I am anxious to mention it, if only to illustrate the extent to which my mind could be distanced from my subsequent worries – the subject, as I was saying, could be summed up as follows: the motor-car, having in the beginning copied the horse-drawn cart, began to imitate the appearance of coleoptera – beetles, maybugs, cockroaches, ladybirds – just as surely as the inspiration for the helicopter came from the dragonfly or the hornet. Trivial, it will be said? Nevertheless I had been engrossed in this research for months, and obtained a great deal of gratification from such superficial pleasures; it was not solely a question of science, but of art, customs, and concern for style; I had prepared pairs of slides to demonstrate the resemblance between certain cars and the insects which could have served as their models; I had even found a film taken from the air, showing the daily life of a modern city; it seemed exclusively populated by colonies of metallic insects.

Thus, everything was ready except the essential, the text of the lecture. I had put aside a Sunday in mid-November, a Sunday when Clarence intended to visit her parents in Sète, to shut myself up from morning to evening and to write. Up at seven, I had nobly gone without breakfast, making do with a spartan coffee-pot on my desk. By eight o'clock I was at my post. I had already written the first paragraph eight times and torn it up eight times, when, at nine o'clock – it had to be on the hour – Vallauris phoned me.

'I have an idea for our investigation. If you could possibly spare a moment during the course of the day . . .'

How could I say no? His action was so exceptional. As I hung up, I cast a glance of jubilant regret at my blank pages, the hypocritical glance of the schoolboy who complains about being disturbed just when he is starting his homework, while thanking heaven like a coward for this providential distraction.

When I drove into his street, André was already waiting for me on the pavement, muffled up in a long white scarf. Winter was early that year.

He got in beside me.

'If, when we get back from this excursion, you feel I've upset your day unjustifiably, don't say anything, I'd be hurt, but forgive me in your heart.'

I put on my most filial smile.

'Which way are we going?'

'Take the Orléans road. A friend is expecting us, a very old friend. Our families were refugees in Geneva, during the Second World War. As boys we were both mad on scientific research. But his father didn't insist on his becoming a lawyer.

'We haven't seen much of each other in recent years, he's mostly lived and worked in California. Now he's spending his retirement peacefully near Orléans, in a large country-house, surrounded by his trees, his books and his grandchildren – paradise on earth! He's devoted his life to the genetic improvement of plants. He's not made any spectacular discoveries, nothing with a pronounceable name, but certain pears which we munch owe their flesh, skin and aroma nearly as much to him as to nature. His subject is one of the most rewarding, since it allows you to keep company with flowers and fruit, and to taste for yourself what you've invented. However, you need years of patience and ingenuity.

'You can guess, we're not going to see him to talk about plants. Ah, but it's a perpetual delight when he does get started on that! But he's not one of those people who make a fetish of water-tight compartments, he likes to cross-fertilize subjects and study their hybrid fruits. Yesterday, on the phone, I told him about my observations. I'm sure his reactions will interest you. As he's a scientist, a genuine one. Not like me, just a Nosey-Parker.'

H

I spoke just now of cars and the similarity I found between them and insects: I ought to have begun by saying the same thing about humans. I don't mean those allegedly similar moral qualities popularized by fables, and which compare such and such a person to an ant, a grasshopper, a bee, a fly or a praying mantis. For my part, I am only speaking of physical likenesses.

In fact, I am in the habit of attaching to people I meet the label of the insects of whose appearance they remind me. Thus – and this is the reason for this somewhat frivolous digression – André's friend immediately made me think of an *agrion virgo* – the damsel-fly – with exceptionally flat antennae . . . I'm not ashamed to write this, since I told him so a few years later, and he laughed and asked me to show him his double. On that occasion I explained that I suffered from a pathological inability to recognize people; that I have occasionally met a colleague in the street whom I saw every day at the Museum, and couldn't place him because I was seeing him out of his usual environment, without his white lab. coat and accompanied by his wife and children; and that with my students my memory was so selective that it played tricks on me: I was capable of remembering, ten years later, the details of a conversation I had had with one of them, and the opinions he'd expressed, without making any mistake with his name; but I might have met this same student in the street an hour after our conversation without recognizing him. As if for me, people had perfectly identifiable moral and intellectual characteristics, whereas their physical characteristics remained indistinct.

After having made countless enemies because of this, I decided one day to have recourse to a mnemonic I invented. Aware that I never mistook the specific characteristics of coleoptera, to the point where I could distinguish at first glance the minutest differences which others could only see with a microscope, and that for thousands of species; having also noticed that every human being had some characteristics which could be associated with a certain species of insect; I now had the solution to my problem: in future I would attach to every individual a sort of coded name for my personal use . . . You are not obliged to take my word for it, but that is how I manage to recognize my pharmacist if I meet her at the baker's.

To get back to André's friend, I haven't yet said that his name was Emmanuel Liev. At the time he was virtually unknown. I can still remember his first words of greeting.

'I'd have liked to show you the trees which are growing old in my company, but our species feels the cold, especially the Vallauris variety; well, André, I could easily see you hibernating in an armchair from November to March. But perhaps I shouldn't talk like this in front of your young friend. Excuse us, my dear sir, I knew André when he was twelve years old and I was fourteen, I used to call him "junior" to annoy him, and I have always had this advantage over him.'

Nothing more natural than that I should feel like an adolescent in the presence of my two seniors. But the way I looked at André must have seemed strange. He stood there beaming, not saying a word, a dumpy stocky figure, as if shrunken, and as I fixed my gaze on him, I could suddenly see the child, the 'junior' of whom his friend spoke; and I realized I had never suspected André of ever being a child, least of all an infant in nappies, having always seen him in his armchair, as if on a pedestal, a sort of timeless sphinx. A few casual slaps on the shoulder had been sufficient for the urchin to emerge from under the adult carapace.

It was not till we were inside the house and he had taken off his coat, then flopped down in the largest armchair, that the vision disappeared and the familiar picture reappeared.

Emmanuel Liev also dropped the playful behaviour reminiscent of his Genevan childhood, his comical expression gave way to a thoughtful smile. Between his eyebrows two deep furrows of wisdom. He began to speak, addressing Vallauris in particular, although he courteously let his eyes wander from one to the other of his guests.

'Since yesterday I've been turning over in my mind all the facts you've collected, and I certainly think your anxieties tie up with some worries I've had for a long time. We're watching the same disease, although we are not necessarily reading the symptoms in the same way.

'Take these famous "boys' nursing-homes" denounced by the Indian doctors; this is a serious matter, and not new since it dates back to the eighties. We are in the presence of a moral dilemma for doctors, parents, and also for the authorities, since such a practice, despicable as it may be, is often perfectly legal. The woman has a scan; it's a girl; she swallows an abortive pill. Neither the mother nor the doctor will admit that this is downright sexual discrimination, on the contrary, they will claim that they are defending the right of the mother to choose. So, a moral dilemma, but of no great consequence up to now, to go by the population figures. Nowadays it is possible to detect the sex of the foetus early enough and with sufficient certainty, but the method is costly. It has only become widespread in rich countries; in the rest, it still only affects a minute fraction of the urban population, the wealthiest and best educated fraction. Among these women, whether it's a question of the large number in rich countries or the élite of poor countries, it can be presumed that the great majority want to know the sex of the child out of legitimate curiosity, simply in order to know, possibly to be able to announce to the father, "It will be a girl", or "a boy", or "triplets". But how many are so anxious to have a child of one particular sex and not of the other, that they would go so far as to have an abortion, even if it were easy, legal and not contrary to their beliefs? Very few, I think. From the moral point of view, the dilemma is the same; but if one is speaking of population figures, I doubt if it is already significant. I know I don't have the proofs to hand, I lightly toss out words like "majority", "many", or "very few", I am nevertheless deeply convinced, as judges say, that the danger lies elsewhere.

An elderly lady arrived, pushing a glass trolley; she was elegant and still so slender that it was impossible to imagine she had been slimmer in her youth. Irene Liev. André kissed her hand and then, after a laugh, her two cheeks.

'I've put your food straight on to your plates. I thought that way you wouldn't notice the frugal menu. I've also brought this wine.'

She sat down beside Emmanuel who put down his glass and plate without tasting anything.

'You and I will start,' she continued, 'the old man can't drink or breathe while he's talking.'

The 'old man' held her wrist affectionately in his horny hand.

'As I was saying, the danger lies elsewhere. I've been certain for some time that it lay in another fact which has intrigued you, André. What is more commonplace than a measles epidemic in Africa in the seventies? Few victims, few after-effects, no echo in the media. But for some scientists, it's like a hurricane!

'It had in fact been ascertained that the women affected by the epidemic nearly always gave birth to boys only. Other observations were collected in different countries for all sorts of epidemics, and the phenomenon began to be a little better understood. I am not sufficiently qualified to explain it to you properly, but the basic idea is that when a woman is fighting the disease, she develops antibodies which attack the foetus she is carrying, as if they confuse it with a virus. They reject it as soon as it is formed and, selectively, certain ones – like the African measles – attack girls in particular, others go for boys. A woman could then, in theory, be immunized against girls and only have boys, or vice versa. There has been continued research and it seems that, at a certain moment, a team got the idea of manufacturing a vaccine. Yes, a vaccine – an injection, a scarification, or perhaps even a tablet. To be sure of having a boy, the woman is "vaccinated" against girls, and no female foetus can develop.

'But allow me to return for a moment to those "boys' nursing homes". I said that the danger was diminished by the fact that they use a costly technique, but also because people who are disappointed in the sex announced to them, generally hesitate to go so far as to interrupt the pregnancy. But if this vaccine is manufactured, widespread, generalized, scanning would no longer be necessary, and there would no longer be the impression of having an abortion. It would be selective contraception, so to speak. In certain countries, in certain societies, the balance of the sexes would not be seriously upset, but on the planet as a whole, it would be a disaster. I don't even dare imagine the consequences.'

He fell silent. Remained thoughtful for a few minutes. Took his first sip of wine. Before managing a slight smile.

'Fortunately, the research has come to a stand-still. Insurmountable technical difficulties, so a colleague explained. Perhaps these will be overcome one day, to our great misfortune. In any case, I am virtually certain that the vaccine has not been manufactured and is not yet near to being. For the last year, I have been reassured on that score. Only, I have other causes for anxiety.'

He gazed into his glass as if he were trying to read the future in it.

'The idea of an anti-girl vaccine is monstrous enough, but an even more monstrous idea has sprung up in some minds.

'It all started with an apparently harmless experiment on bovines. Several years ago, it was discovered that it was possible in the course of artificial insemination in the laboratory, to act on the bulls' sperm to favour either male or female births, according to one's preference; a method perfectly applicable moreover to other species, including our own. Then they wondered if there might not be a way of treating the animal directly by inoculating it with a substance which would modify its offspring. The research has progressed relatively fast. A substance has been perfected which considerably increases the bulls' potency and fertility, which as it were "dopes" the spermatazoa responsible for male births, so as to make any female birth extremely unlikely.

'The result was the opposite of what was intended, since the initial idea was rather to help the breeders to obtain a greater number of cows, more profitable for dairy products and reproduction. So the majority of researchers thought they ought to shelve the discovery, for the good reason that the animals treated became dangerously aggressive. But some smart fellows thought it could be turned to advantage, in particular for bull-fighting. And even to adapt the substance for other species of fighting animals, such as dogs or cocks.

'And why not humans one day? Not only produce monsters for the ring, but – as with the "vaccine" – satisfy, in hundreds of millions of families, the ancestral desire, the "obligation", to have a son?

'At this stage, before this project was too far advanced, someone intervened. Certain biologists were said to be nervous and to have alerted well-known scientists, members of the Académie Française, bishops, politicians; I say "were said to be" since I only know snatches of what went on, I don't know any names, or even the country where the laboratory was situated, although I have my suspicions. But that is not important. The main thing is that a decision was made and action discreetly taken. The project was interrupted, the funds allocated to something else and the team disbanded.

'Since then, whenever I hear about these questions of selective births, I prick up my ears. For the knowledge exists, there is an enormous potential market, and so many of our fellow-creatures are blinded by the lure of profit. How is it possible not to feel disquiet?'

'To listen to you, the situation seems unavoidable.'

Emmanuel Liev took advantage of my worried remark to swallow another noisy sip of red wine. Before shaking his head.

'My friend André, like me, will tell you that all villainies are possible, but none is inevitable if one keeps careful watch. To answer your question more directly, it is true that as far as the knowledge is concerned, it is doubtless possible to manufacture this damnable substance today, and has perhaps been possible since the mid-nineties. One day, I am convinced, it will in fact be available. The whole thing is to know when. The whole thing is to know if it will come at a time when men and women are sufficiently mature to use it in a responsible manner. Who am I, you will ask, to speak of my fellow-creatures as if they were minors? I would reply that I am an old codger of seventy-three and over the years I've had the opportunity of observing the way the human race uses the most modern means in the service of the most hackneyed causes. The weapons of 2000 are used to settle conflicts which date back to the year 1000. Formidable energy is discovered in the atom, and it's used to make exterminating mushrooms. And if this "substance" were manufactured, would it not be the fruit of long labours using the most refined techniques? And to what use would it be put? To eliminate millions and millions of girls on all five continents because a stupid tradition, dating back to the age of the cudgel, demands that the family be perpetuated through sons. Once again, the modern instrument at the service of an outmoded cause.

'Yes, I know, mentalities evolve in the same way as

techniques, they drag each other along, follow in each other's footsteps. But they don't always proceed at the same pace. Sometimes, when danger threatens, we must try to slow down the advance of techniques, or their proliferation. In 1945, as soon as the atomic bomb became operational, it was used without the slightest thought for the consequences; it claimed hundreds of thousands of victims without modifying the outcome of the war, at most it shortened the battle in the Pacific by a few months. If it had been available in 1943, Hitler would have used it against London, then Moscow, New York and Washington, the course of history would have been upset and our families, my poor André, would not even have been safe in Switzerland. I'm not saying anything new here; I simply want to insist on the time factor. I'd have preferred the bomb never to have been manufactured, or if it had to be, then in two hundred years' time; but I'm glad it didn't come two years earlier. I also appreciate the fact that it has remained a cumbersome, costly technology and if there is proliferation, it is extremely slow. It's the same thing with this damnable substance. If it only becomes widespread in thirty years time, I dare to hope that mankind will not abuse it. But today? Just look at the world we are living in!'

I confess that at the time I could only guess very vaguely what he was alluding to; I cast a sidelong glance at André, who was nodding his beard with a stricken air; then I glanced at Irene Liev who asked, 'Ought there not to have been intervention sooner, to cut short the research which was clearly leading to this disastrous result?'

'That's the sort of thing one says with hindsight, but at the time no scientist wants the authorities, whoever they may be, to come sticking their noses in his test-tubes. Our young friend here will confirm this. And then the research itself is not in question. You don't take all four wheels off a car to prevent it skidding. Isn't is simpler to alter the way we drive?

'Let me take an example from my speciality. There is, among my colleagues, a man who has spent twenty years of his career creating heavier and heavier varieties of apple, which have no flavour and less nutritive value than the ones we are in the habit of eating, and whose sole merit is to earn more money for unscrupulous farmers.

'I have another colleague, a Venetian woman, who has succeeded, after thirty years of trials, in doubling the volume of a certain variety of rice, while concentrating its vitamin content; today, nearly two hundred million human beings have an improved food supply, thanks to her.

'Well, these two researchers have studied the same books, used the same basic discoveries, the same techniques. Only they haven't made the same use of them.'

I

When I got back to Paris, I settled down at my desk without
delay, not to resume writing out my lecture, but to transcribe
word for word what Liev had said, before it lost its freshness
in the stress of my week's activities. I'd no idea at the time
that one day I would write this book of my reminiscences; I
just wanted to offer Clarence, on paper, some material
which might help her investigations. Had I not promised her
she could count on my fraternal collaboration?

When she returned home from Sète about midnight, she
reacted exactly as I had hoped, down to the last flicker of an
eyelash. Grasping my pages in both hands, at the risk of
crushing them, she began to pace up and down the room,
barefoot, while I watched her steadily. Then she simply said,
'This time!' And flung herself down across the bed.

This time, yes, there was ample material to investigate.
True, there were no names, places, dates, but the task did not
frighten her, she would work her way through all the
channels, get people to talk, filch documents if need be. At
her paper, there were going to be some gloomy faces!

That's what I had in mind, you'll say – Clarence's revenge
on the people at the paper who'd laughed at her. But what of
the danger itself? And the millions of girls who would not be
allowed to be born, victims of the discriminatory "substance"? Naturally, I was thinking of that, but if it had not

been for my companion, I would not have taken the trouble to transcribe three hours' conversation. I felt that the fears expressed by Liev, and which Vallauris seemed to share, were, if I may say so, worthy of respect rather than a cause for alarm. It all arose, apparently, from an intellectual exercise on the part of a decent chap, one Sunday in a country house in Orléannais. If we had been talking in equally alarming terms about the atom, drugs, the spread of Aids, the melting of the polar ice-cap, I would have been interested, intrigued, moved, perturbed; without necessarily feeling more concerned than billions of my fellow-men. I won't go so far as to say that my companion's career was more important to me than the fate of the world, but I behaved as if this were the case. Who will throw the first stone? Are the causes of other people's sleepless nights any more significant?

The editor was not delighted to hear a subject mentioned again that she had thought definitely buried beneath mockery. However, she had to take account of the new elements which seemed to justify Clarence's persistence.

'We'll come to a decision next Monday when the editorial committee meets. Meanwhile, to be sure neither of us is led off on a wild goose chase, I'd like you to go and see Pradent.'

Need I introduce Pradent? Nowadays he has doubtless been somewhat forgotten, but at that time he was so well known, had been so long in the public eye, that his name had become a by-word. I even think he had been in the government for a short period, but I'd have to go through all the lists to find out when and which portfolio he held. At the time I'm speaking of, he was the chairman of several committees, several associations, and 'adviser' to Clarence's paper, of which he was an important shareholder. A man of power and an opinion-maker.

Clarence was quite prepared to meet him – had she any choice? – but the day before the appointment she was rather on edge. She would have been quite at ease confronting any of the great men of this world as long as he was in his normal role and she in hers; but on going to see Pradent, she felt she was peddling her wares. She didn't like that and, what is more, she didn't feel sufficiently competent on the subject. I suggested I accompany her, since I had talked directly to Liev, but she proudly shrugged off my offer.

Pradent proved friendly, reassuring, and allowed his visitor to explain the subject of her proposed investigation without interruption, simply encouraging her from time to time by an understanding nod. She kept close to the facts, nevertheless she refrained from referring to Liev or Vallauris by name or mentioning the word 'scarab' for fear of this being the excuse for some sarcasm. But Pradent had been informed.

'Muriel Vaast tells me that you have certain Egyptian capsules in your possession.'

'The scarab beans. I didn't mention them as there's no proof that they have any connection with this business.'

'One never knows! What did you call them? "Scarab beans", I've already seen those words somewhere, but at my age, one's memory . . .'

He fell silent, screwed up his eyes, and Clarence waited respectfully for him to finish racking his brains and to resume.

'I'll try to remember. But let's get back to what you've told me. My first reaction, before having time to reflect, is that this is all very confused, very vague. The only apparently tangible fact, which I presume you have confirmed, is the imbalance in the birthrate of boys and girls in certain countries. However these are phenomena which can only be studied scientifically after a decade, not before. Anyway, let's suppose that what you've been told has some basis in fact. Mind you, I don't think it will happen, but let's suppose that one day a simple and efficacious method of reducing the birthrate in certain parts of the world is discovered. Would that constitute a disaster or genocide? I don't think so. There are over-populated countries which can no longer manage to feed themselves; their governments have tried all sorts of ways of controlling the demographic explosion, with limited results, and sometimes none at all. If tomorrow, or even today, a method could be found to reduce the birthrate without violence, without force, with the free consent of the parents . . .'

By the expression in the eyes of his visitor, Pradent must have seen that his argument had carried. He looked at her hard and straight.

'Yes, if such a solution were found, in what way would it be criminal or scandalous? When China wanted to impose one child per family, many parents in Shanghai and elsewhere bribed doctors and nurses to get rid of the first child if it was a girl; in India, when they wanted to enforce sterilization, there were riots; men had the impression they were losing their virility, their honour. If the substance you are speaking of were perfected, the same result could be expected without hurting the feelings of these people, even agreeing with them.'

Clarence looked as if she had suddenly woken up from a long hypnotic sleep.

'If I understand correctly, whole populations will in effect be sterilized, even when every individual feels potent and fertile and, what is more, will have the pleasure of having two, three, four boys.'

'It's not a question of sterilizing whole populations, but we cannot ignore the fact that, if such a substance existed, and became widespread, the problem of over-population would eventually be resolved in areas where it is most acute.

'Look at the world today. It is clearly divided into two. On the one hand, societies with a stable population, getting richer and richer, more and more democratic, with a new technical breakthrough practically every day, life expectancy endlessly improving, a veritable golden age of unprecedented peace, freedom, prosperity, progress, without any precedent in History. On the other hand, larger and larger populations growing endlessly poorer, with sprawling cities where food has to be shipped in, nations falling into chaos one after the other.

'For decades people have been searching for solutions, but every day the problem becomes more serious. There are two races and the gap between them has become impossible to bridge. If suddenly providence sent a solution, who would complain? Would the rulers of the Third World complain, when they have endlessly to feed more and more new mouths, while watching the faint progress in production wiped out, swept away, drowned in the demographic flood? And we, the privileged ones, in a smaller and smaller minority, don't we wish our fellow creatures in the South were a little more prosperous and a little less numerous? Who would complain, tell me, if a solution were found?'

In actual fact Clarence could not see, could not yet see, who could have reason to complain. Pradent's argument seemed for the moment to have a crushing logic. Then she tried, by a healthy reflex, to bring the discussion back on to ground where she felt herself better able to hold her own.

'I'm very impressed by what you say, I admit this in all simplicity, and I shall think it over long after I've left you. You have put your finger on a basic problem of our times. And just because it is a basic problem, it would be normal for our paper to discuss it, and devote more space to it than I imagined when I entered your office.'

'I'm glad my words have touched you. But these are only opinions; and they've been in the air for a long time, there's nothing new in them. If one day you want to deal with the problems of the Third World, come and see me, I shall have many more things to tell you. Meanwhile, I must make it clear that in this friendly conversation I have only been thinking aloud about an abstract hypothesis which you have put to me, namely the existence of a substance permitting the selection of the sex of a child. To the best of my knowledge such a substance does not exist. If it were being distributed today throughout the world, from India to Egypt, do you think the matter could have remained secret?'

He glanced furtively at his watch to indicate to Clarence that the conversation could not be prolonged any further. However, she insisted.

'I'm prepared to believe that this story has no basis, but I would like to complete my investigation.'

Pradent rose quickly to his feet.

'I understand your persistence, I was young and obstinate myself once. But take an old man's word for it, you would be wasting your time.'

'Still, may I conduct my investigation? May I tell Muriel Vaast that you've got nothing against it?'

'My dear young lady, there's some misunderstanding. You came to ask my advice, I advised you to the best of my ability, my responsibility stopped there. If you wish to proceed with your investigation, you should discuss it with your editor.'

As he showed her to the door, he added with a slightly hypocritical smile, 'In any case, as soon as I have any material which may clarify the situation, I'll send it to you. To you or Madame Vaast.'

I have been able to report the tenor of the conversation in this way because, as you will have guessed, Clarence gave me a faithful account of it as soon as she got back. However, when she finished, she added thoughtfully and with an air of being dissatisfied, 'Now you know what Pradent said, but I think I have left out the most important thing.'

She fell silent, searching for words, or for some image fresh in her memory.

'I've no proof, but as I watched his face twitching and caught a hesitation in his voice, especially when he mentioned the "substance", I was convinced he was speaking of something which does exist, not simply of a hypothesis. In spite of all his verbal precautions.'

She reflected again.

'I also had a curious impression when he mentioned the "sacrab beans" . . .'

When, two days later, at the editorial committee meeting, Clarence began to speak of her plan again, there were a few smiles, but she did not take offence, concentrating on presenting the most striking evidence in her file, in particular the material Vallauris had collected. Muriel Vaast let her develop her argument before asking, 'You've seen Pradent, haven't you? What does he think?'

'He thinks the problem deserves our interest, but that the facts available so far are still insufficient.'

'If I've understood correctly, he considers that we're floundering in pure speculation.'

Clarence made as if to reply; her editor silenced her with a reassuring gesture.

'I admit there are some aspects which may reasonably excite one's curiosity. Like these scarab beans – do you honestly believe they have any connection with the phenomenon you're studying?'

'I must explore every avenue. And that one most of all.'

'I'm under the impression that you mentioned them to Pradent . . .'

'He said the name rang a bell but he couldn't quite remember what it was.'

'Well, he did remember. This morning he sent us this.'

Muriel Vaast took a leather-bound book out of her brief-case and began to read: ' "My companions and I entered one of the booths that serve as pharmacies in this little town. We were offered Turkish compresses, balsams which would have stunk our ship out for the rest of the voyage, as well as the famous 'scarab beans' whose aphrodisiac virtues had recently been vaunted to us; we all refused them, some of us out of distrust, others out of discretion." The title of this book is *My Voyage on the Nile*, by Gustave Meissonier. It was published in . . .' (she turned the pages, taking her time quite conspicuously about verifying) '. . . in Marseilles in 1904.'

*

Buried, the scarab.

But what can I say about Clarence? About her wounded susceptibilities? Her hurt feelings? Her lifeless eyes?

Completely crushed.

I would have liked her to scream, shout abuse, slam a door or break an ugly lamp. No, not even the strength to wipe away a tear from the end of her nose. I only learned from confused snatches what had happened: the trap, the crescendo of laughter, the colleague who apologized for a fit of hiccups between two choking attacks. She had stopped her ears, run away, rushed down the stairs, sobbed in the taxi. Once back at the flat, she had collapsed. Until my return.

I was not averse to playing the part of comforter, had I not been so anxious about Clarence. In the following days, I was frequently reminded of a scene in a Polish film from the seventies. A journalist complains bitterly to a psychoanalyst friend about the worries of his profession which made his life a misery. 'Tell yourself,' his friend replies, 'that the only serious thing that can happen is for you to lose your instinct for self-preservation.' That was exactly what I feared for my journalist-consort: depression, instability, sinking into an abyss. For the rest of the week I took sick leave, to be able to hold her hand.

'Don't dwell on it, don't chew it over, spit out the poisons instead of letting them circulate in your body!'

My treatment was simple: my presence, affectionate chit-chat, and interminable breakfasts in the bay window. So we lingered for whole days sipping our coffee, nibbling, exchanging the most delightful nonsense, and when the silence was sometimes prolonged, I talked about insects. I had stored up hundreds of ancedotes and each one pulled out another, like paper handkerchiefs.

Soon her tears dried, but Clarence remained listless, lack-lustre. She said she was incapable of setting foot at the paper again and I encouraged her to resign. Either for a different one where she would be more appreciated, or – I only hinted – to take long leave in the course of which Beatrice would be born.

'Given the state I'm in, she'd be a very sad little girl. I'd have liked to stop work at the height of my fame, radiant, victorious, I'd have liked the baby to come as the crowning point of my happiness, not like a consolation prize, not as a cure for depression.'

'Why do you say "cure"? If by her birth, she helped you over this bad patch, wouldn't the baby be more of an ally, an accomplice? For my part, I'd even call her your "salvation"!'

She looked at me curiously, and I detected in her eyes a sort of affectionate lack of understanding. Then she exclaimed, with a mock swagger, 'If I say yes one day, it will be because I love you.'

'I don't know any better reason.'

It was already a 'yes'.

She made the announcement on the day I was to give my public lecture on the motor-car and coleoptera. I had still not found time for the necessary hours of concentration to write out the text, and I had made up my mind to go in with notes jotted down on a folded card; I often did this for my lectures to students, but when the audience was different and the subject less familiar I avoided counting too much on my presence of mind.

So I had slept badly, and woken up in a terrible state, my brain was one huge black hole, I was going off to the slaughter-house . . . Just as I was leaving, Clarence whispered to me – although we were completely alone – that she 'would stop taking precautions.'

There was unanimous acknowledgement that, on that Wednesday, I had spoken brilliantly, convincingly, that I had shown a rare mastery of the subject and undeniable qualities as an orator . . . I shook dozens of hands, repeating to myself, with every compliment I received, 'Thank you Clarence,' 'Thank you Beatrice.'

And that evening, when I put my arms round my companion's waist, we felt we were going to bed for the first time.

As I undressed her, she asked me teasingly, 'Is it me you love or your daughter?'

'I love the whole world at this moment, but I want to express it to your body.'

She pretended to slip away.

'You'll be to blame, in a few months time, for my body becoming shapeless.'

'Shapeless, a belly growing round like the earth? Shapeless, breasts flowing with milk, offering their brown lips to the infant's lips, arms which clasp flesh to flesh, and this face bent over the babe? God! It's the most beautiful picture that any mortal can contemplate. Come!'

That is the moment when, in discreet films, a lamp is extinguished, a door closes, a curtain falls. And in some books a page is turned, but slowly, as these minutes should turn, slowly, and with no other sound than the rustle of a sheet.

Beatrice was born on the last night of August, a little before term, as if to catch up with the beginning of the school
year, a model pupil, but already inclined to be rowdy,
insomniac and greedy, waving her feet in the air to signal
endless indecipherable semaphore messages. A curious pink
insect.

The following morning, alone in the flat, shaven, sweet-
smelling, humming a tune, I was getting ready to go to the
maternity home to meet the two women in my life, when I
received the most unexpected phone call. Muriel Vaast. She
would like to speak to Clarence.

Muriel Vaast! The rare occasions when her name still
came up in our conversations it was like a tin target on a
fairground stall. But this was not the moment for old
grudges, it was Beatrice's moment and my voice was almost
friendly.

'Clarence is not here just now.'

'Excuse me, but is she still living at this address?'

'More than ever!'

I'm not sure whether my cry of joy was addressed to the
right audience. She cleared her throat, apparently disturbed
by this sort of familiarity.

'I'd have liked a few words with her.'

'I can ask her to return your call when she gets back.'

'No, I'm not sure she would do that. Could you give her a message from me . . .?'

'If you like, I can record it.'

'Yes, perhaps that would be best.'

I switched on the answering machine.

'Dear Clarence. I've been wanting for some time to offer you my apologies – a bit late, but quite sincere. This summer, I've often had another think about . . . No, listen, I feel very awkward, I'd rather drop her a line.'

'Just as you like.'

This remorse surfacing ten months too late struck me as a trifle suspect. Clarence's loud expression of disgust was justified two days later when the daily papers gave priority to a report by the United Nations on the 'discriminatory birth rate' an expression which was, alas! to enjoy a lasting vogue!

According to the authors of this report – some ten or so experts from various countries – a significant decline in female births had been recorded 'without it being possible to attribute this to any one cause'. There was rather – here, however, the report remained vague – 'a collection of independent factors which could have apparently combined to produce this distortion.' It quoted in particular 'the generalized spread of abortions of a discriminatory nature, the propagation of certain methods of increasing fertility selectively . . .' The phenomenon was said to have become considerably worse in the course of the last four years, affecting every continent, although not to the same degree.

Before going into more detail about the ensuing debate, I must admit that it constantly gave me cause for surprise, sometimes pleasant, sometimes unpleasant, and often baffled me. Is it on account of the time I spend with coleoptera that I find myself so ignorant and naïve when it comes to human beings? I'd have imagined the report would awaken the survival reflex; it merely gave rise to quarrels among the specialists. I won't go so far as to allege that my fellow-creatures are lacking in a certain instinct for survival, as individuals, as groups; and, to a lesser degree, as a species. Nevertheless, our natures are too complex for such an instinct to be a constant guide for our actions; it gets lost in a dark forest of ideas, sensations, impulses, which assert their priority, with the result that they mask the need for survival. Moreover, this is not unknown among certain insects, as I shall doubtless have the opportunity of explaining.

At this point in my story, I should simply like to put on record that, after the publication of the report, it was much talked about, but every time it was discussed the confusion grew greater, the warning it contained became less audible, less credible. After a few days, everything the experts had said seemed simultaneously true, false, basic and superfluous. The outcome was insignificant. Were we not living in the age of blinding enlightenment?

As I remember it, this debate remains linked to Beatrice's birth. A new age was beginning for my tiny tribe, but perhaps also for the rest of humanity. When our 'guest' woke us up at night, every night, and several times a night, Clarence and I had got into the curious habit of both getting up together, Clarence to feed her, me – will you believe it? – to read to Clarence, in an undertone, articles on her subject, which helped us get through this period without undue anxiety; it is true, we were both on leave since my lectures did not begin in theory until October, and I had asked to be relieved of all teaching until the end of the first term.

It was not exactly the sabbatical I had promised Clarence, but her own leave was to be still shorter. In the first days of November she put an end to this enforced idleness; after two false starts, she was impatient to embark at last on her investigation.

'I'm leaving you and your daughter,' she exclaimed one day, with a laugh of liberation, her hand on the door handle.

Then she was off on her travels.

Her first visit took her, on my recommendation, to Orléannais, to see Emmanuel Liev. But I very soon lost track of her. In between taking two showers, she would shout that she was leaving for Rome or Casa or Zurich; two days later a scribbled note would inform me she had come home 'to change', then left again. This merry-go-round continued for three weeks. Muriel Vaast phoned nearly every day, but Clarence had an agreement with a large-circulation daily which had already advanced all the expenses for the investigation.

Her article appeared in December, shortly before Christmas, and I have the impression it contained the first serious information on the emergence of the tragedy. I am not speaking here as a lover, but as a scientist, and an indefatigable reader. I had collected everything published in the world press. André, for his part, had swamped me with cuttings, and I can certify that, before Clarence's investigation, there was still only a small amount of scattered facts and hypotheses. Thanks to the precise indications supplied by Liev, she had been able to proceed further.

In the first place, she was able to confirm, with proofs, that a team of researchers, encouraged by the success of certain experiments on bovines, had tried to perfect a substance capable of acting on the genital organs of the father, in order to favour masculine births. High authorities had in fact intervened, the team had indeed been penalized and disbanded, but the project was already sufficiently advanced to be taken up in other laboratories, in countries where the authorities were less fussy.

One man in particular had undertaken the double task of producing and distributing the 'substance' – a certain Dr Foulbot, today sadly notorious, who was the real commercial brain of the team after having been unsuccessful as the scientific brain. He was the one who soon had the idea of settling abroad, taking over, in various countries in the South, certain companies which had long been manufacturing psuedo-pharmaceutical products and using their labels to sell his new product.

One of these companies, based in a Red Sea port, had been manufacturing scarab beans for two hundred years. Clarence made it her business to tell how Dr Foulbot had acquired it in the nineties, and expanded it into an unobtrusive but enormous multinational.

'This man had the brilliant idea of selling a revolutionary substance under an old label, being careful not to say this aloud, so as not to arouse the suspicion of the authorities. Scarab beans and similar products have never been perfectly legal, but they were tolerated, and a network of vendors had been distributing them as long as anyone could remember, to a vast number of gullible customers. To these, Foulbot was suddenly bringing, without any fuss, a genuinely efficacious, well-nigh infallible product; he had gambled on word of mouth being sufficient to spread the reputation of his goods fairly quickly; he had just belatedly discovered the already old virtues of the product, whereas the authorities, used to seeing these same allegedly miraculous powders always available, would be completely taken in. As a final precaution – taken, it seems, after the first articles in the press mentioned the "scarab" – Foulbot found it necessary to use different labels and vary the packaging.'

It appeared that the 'substance' had been widely distributed for seven years, particularly in countries in the South, and under countless different names, allowing Foulbot, as may easily be imagined, to amass a colossal fortune.

Wisely Clarence avoided expounding on the possible consequences of the large-scale use of the 'substance', only referring to this aspect of the matter in general terms in the final paragraph and, for the rest, simply presenting the facts and firmly establishing their credibility.

Moreover, thanks to her, and some subsequent investigations largely inspired by hers, certain truths were no longer questioned: namely the existence of the said 'substance', its wide distribution, the general complacency about it. What, on the other hand, was bitterly debated, and for many years, could be reduced to two successive questions: would the 'substance' have a deep and lasting influence on the population of the world? And, if such was the case, would this development be, all in all, beneficial or harmful?

I would prefer not to enlarge on this debate; it is too easy to analyse, with hindsight, the different predictions and to distribute good marks and bad. No one, in this affair, was an infallible prophet; but some were less blind than others. Such as Clarence. However, I think it by no means superfluous to devote three or four paragraphs to an opinion which went the rounds and which was prevalent for some time. No one expressed it more clearly than Paul Pradent in an article published only a few days after Clarence's and entitled, 'A New Population for the New Millennium'. In it he repeated and enlarged on certain ideas he had expressed in his interview with her.

'Not for the first time,' he said, 'do we find ourselves presented with absurd scenarios, based on a few statistics, and developing in a farcical manner a tendency that is scarcely visible. How many times has the end of the world been announced? But the Earth is a difficult egg to crack.'

Then, after a short digression, and a clear reference to my companion: 'We are told that substances have recently been perfected which could have the effect of slowing down the growth of the world population. Rather than drawing imaginary graphs to warn us about depopulation, why should we not, on the contrary, see here a normal and welcome stage in the history of the world?

'For thousands of years, in fact, the world population has only increased slowly and erratically; when births were very numerous, then deaths were no less so; infantile mortality, epidemics, wars, famine, prevented too great an increase. Then we entered a new phase, in the course of which the death rate fell thanks to the progress of medicine and agricultural techniques; yet, still moving on its own momentum, the birth rate remained high. However this phase could not continue indefinitely. Logically, the birth rate had to decline, so that the world population could resume a controlled, harmonious stability. This has been the case for several decades in the developed countries, which, because of this, enjoy peace and prosperity. Is it not desirable that it should be the same everywhere? Is not the present situation wrong, namely that the countries which can feed, clothe, care for and educate their children have fewer and fewer, while those which are unable to look after them have more and more?

'If, by some miracle, the surplus population in poor countries was to be reduced, we should see violence, famine, barbarism disappear in one generation. Mankind would finally be ripe to enter the new millennium.'

And Pradent concluded with this formula which, the more one thinks about it, seems comical, to say the least: 'Let us leave it to the workings of nature!'

Despite this blunder in the last line (the 'substance', the workings of nature?) the argument was not easy to refute and I understand that it could have been attractive. For my part, when I finished reading, I shrugged my shoulders. Pradent's logic was indisputable. But I am a complicated animal. The simpler the logic, the more suspicious I become. I don't always know why I am suspicious, something in my training makes me see the flea on the elephant's back even before I see the elephant; something in my sensibilities distances me from ideas which claim to be unanimous.

For a long time there had also been the influence of André Vallauris. When we were together, in his drawing-room, re-thinking the world, he always encouraged me to brush aside pervading ideas, 'just as one brushes aside the peel of a fruit, delicately out of consideration for the fruit, but without any consideration for the peel.'

O tempera! O mores! Once, people would have hooted with laughter at a couple where the father blossoms through the child and the mother through her work and fame. But that was how it was with us, and we were happy; was I any the less a man for all that, was she any the less a woman?

Yet my happiness was more tangible than Clarence's. From February onwards, every morning, when I left for the Museum, I would leave Beatrice with the baby-minder I had found for her, a widowed neighbour, a grandmother several times over. She lived in a mezzanine flat, and as soon as I set foot on the first stair my daughter clasped me round the neck, a brown garland whose weight and fragrance remained with me all day.

Clarence did her job as a mother with professional efficiency, with the necessary affection, but without any extra fuss. It was understood that the child was a loving gift from her to me; she had promised it, she had given it, with her whole body, and much sooner than I had hoped. I never complained, I never tried to keep her lingering about too long over the cradle. Her path was elsewhere and she followed it.

Since the publication of her investigation, few journalists, men or women, were more appreciated, more in demand, or better remunerated. She, who dreamed of in-depth articles, received more propositions than she could ever manage to undertake. She would pick and choose, often turning offers down, liking to work slowly, patiently polishing, careful, to use her own expression, 'to preserve my scarcity value'. I found her judicious hard-to-get attitude perfectly reasonable and approved of her decision to remain free-lance, concluding selective contracts with one newspaper then another, including the one with which she had made her début and to which she bore no ill-will.

I was, all in all, her sole lasting commitment. Proof against any crises, shocks – and any idea of marriage. We had mentioned it once only, at the beginning of our relationship. I had told her I hankered after the times when the most serious agreements were sealed with a handshake and lasted a lifetime, long after all official documents had grown yellow. Between Clarence and me it was a rather special handshake, more elaborate, more comprehensive, prolonged; but in my mind it was, first and foremost, a handshake. We would remain together as long as our love lasted; and we would use a thousand adolescent ruses to make it last.

We lived in this way, not husband and wife, not a conventional couple, nor concubines . . . What terrible words! We lived as lovers, with life giving us all we could wish for, were it not for the physical wear and tear of age; were it not, also, for the upheavals in the world.

Others than Clarence would have considered they had 'arrived'. She thought this word insulting. 'It should be reserved for railway stations and airports. When I am told that a person has arrived, I'm tempted to ask where, and by what means, and for what purpose!' Was this modesty? I would say, rather, that it was that mixture of modesty and pride known as 'decency'. For she also used to say, 'the only people who congratulate themselves on having arrived are those who know they are incapable of going any further.'

Clarence owed it to herself to follow every trace of the affair which had caused her name and talent to be known; it was now her cause, her life's struggle, and the turn events were taking worried her. When she had published her investigation into the 'substance', she had, it is true, maintained a neutral tone in order to retain her credibility. But her aim was clear: to point out the greed and cynicism of certain sorcerer's apprentices. In this gigantic manipulation of people, in the way the worst was being brought out of people who were being lured towards the goal of a supposedly better future, along the short-cut of systematic discrimination, she obviously saw things sliding out of control to an unacceptable and criminal degree. She reckoned that all she had to do was to reveal the facts for the whole world to be shaken with righteous anger.

Nothing of the kind. I have quoted Pradent's article at length, because I had kept it, and because it had the merit of clarity; I must add that many other key figures from all walks of life came to add their weight to this point of view.

Clarence and I needed time to appreciate the real, profound, and sometimes passionate attraction that ideas like Pradent's exerted on the widest public opinion. We had become accustomed to seeing our most serious worries originate from countries in the South; if a simple solution existed, which could at one and the same time settle their problems and our own, it would be madness not to apply it!

We cannot judge these things with hindsight, we have to put ourselves back, to some extent, into the spirit of the times. Without wishing to linger over the euphoria of the last years of the past century, I would like to emphasize the fact that, as the two wings of the developed world joined, and the gap between their values, institutions, language, way of life closed, so the deep gap which divided the world, the 'horizontal fault-line' responsible for so many tremors, had been thrown into violent relief. On the one side of the divide, all the wealth, all the freedom, all the hope. On the other, a maze of dead-ends: stagnation, violence, rage and storms, spreading an epidemic of chaos, and salvation through a massive exodus to the paradise of the North.

On both sides of this 'fault-line' growing impatience could be sensed. Here, too, it was Vallauris who made me aware of this fact. I can no longer recall the exact events which brought up the subject, nor what I might have said, but it was a question, I think, of religious fanaticism.

André had said, 'Like you, I sometimes get impatient, I explode, storm, vituperate. But immediately afterwards I reason with myself, saying: we must suffer the world as it has suffered us.

'The West has not always been as you have known it, this haven of peace, justice, concerned for the rights of men, women and the natural world. I am a generation older than you, and I have known a very different West. Tell yourself that for centuries we have scoured the Earth, built empires, demolished civilizations, massacred the American Indians, then transported Blacks by the shipload to work in their place, waged war on the Chinese to force them to buy opium, yes, we have swept through the world like a tornado, sometimes a beneficial tornado, but constantly bringing destruction.

'And here, in Europe, what have we done? We have

frantically butchered, bombed, gassed each other wholesale, right up to the middle of the twentieth century. Then, one day, when we'd had enough, when we'd grown weary, older and wiser, we settled down in our most comfortable armchairs, shouting to nobody in particular, "Now, quieten down everyone!" Well, no, you see, everyone doesn't quieten down at the same time as us. Everywhere there are other Alsace-Lorraines, other quarrels between Papists and Huguenots, just as ridiculous as ours were, just as deadly; folly must have its day.

'We must be patient with the world!'

But that was André . . . Patience was to become a rare commodity because of mistakes on both sides; on both sides of the divide, the wisest voices fell silent. Only people belonging to other times, the Vallaurises, the Lievs, could hold out for long against the attraction of a miracle solution.

Public opinion seesawed visibly from one extreme to another. The inventers of the 'substance', who not long since had been hunted down, reduced to silence, were now in a fair way to seeming like benefactors of the whole human race. They were not mistaken, since one day, as everyone will remember, they emerged from the shadows like members of the Resistance the day after the Liberation. Beginning with Dr Foulbot, who came to claim, in exclusive and loquacious interviews, credit for 'the invention of the century' – and in a sense that was what it was – and demand recognition as a 'saviour', long misunderstood like all saviours, persecuted by obscure, retrogade forces, driven into exile.

I can still see him on the box; his eyes flashing from behind the barricade of his thick dark glasses. Why had he not perfected a substance favouring the birth of girls? 'I had begun to work on this when our funds were cut off!' Is it true that he had made a fortune selling his product? 'The money I have managed to earn simply serves to finance my research. I am first and foremost a scientist.' Is he not worried about the discriminatory attitudes resulting from his invention? 'It is in the nature of every drug to be beneficial if utilized judiciously, and dangerous in the contrary case. An inventor must presume that mankind is adult; otherwise many things would have to be disinvented! But science does not function in reverse, mankind can never get rid of its knowledge or its power. That is the way it is, those who would like to live in the past must make the best of it!'

A serious sign of the times, in pharmacies in several Northern countries, certain drugs gradually began to appear, containing the 'substance' and now carrying the label, not of some back-street workshop, but of important pharmaceutical companies, anxious not to leave such a promising market to others. To get round the law against sexual discrimination, these products were presented as remedies for male sterility. So, on condition that they were sold only on a doctor's prescription, the Food and Drugs Administration authorized their distribution in the United States, soon to be followed by the majority of equivalent institutions.

As might have been expected, there was no lack of learned pens to explain that these drugs sold to Northern consumers were radically different from 'scarab beans' and other products of a similar nature. I wouldn't like to let myself be dragged into too technical a discussion; human biology is not my field, pharmacology still less so; besides, everything that I could say here can be found, clearly explained, in specialist publications. For my part, I am only interested in the ensuing troubles, such as I experienced them, and in anything that can help to explain their genesis. If I have lingered over what was being said in the first years of the age of Beatrice, it is to explain that the 'substance' was accepted henceforth as a fact of life, providential for some, regrettable for others, but one manages to co-exist, does one not, with other regrettable facts of life. The debate was closed, save for a handful of obstinate people, and Clarence herself would have wearied her public and lost her credit if she had endlessly returned to an 'out-dated' question.

In any case, that was what she explained to me one day of extreme depression: 'You must think of public opinion as some bulky individual lying asleep. From time to time, he wakes up with a start, and you must take advantage of this to whisper an idea in his ear, but only the simplest, most concise idea, for he's already stretching himself, turning over, yawning, he's going to fall asleep again and you won't be able to keep him awake or awaken him again.

'So, you begin to wait, perversely, for something to jolt his bed.'

L

It's an understatement to say that people's beds were jolted.

There were first a few modest, distant tremors, practically undetectable. I witnessed one of them, due to a mistake on Clarence's part, which I forgave.

It occasionally happened that my partner, on her return from some country with a melodious name, decided to return there with me for her next holiday, without having to worry about any investigation, to savour at leisure the serene delights which she had scarcely tasted. Usually, her enthusiasms did not survive other enthusiasms, one dream was superimposed on another, like coloured, compressed, hardened sediments, Chittagong, Battambang, Mandalay, Djenné, Gonaïves, each one a perfect Paradise.

However, on this occasion, her memories proved more durable. She had been to Naïputo, to report on some international conference or other, such as were popular at the time, with two hundred delegations, each arriving with its pennant, its folklore, its formality, its prepared speech, and the brave hope of catching the ear of these thousands of diplomats, experts, journalists ... This by way of explaining that Clarence, who had arrived late, had the greatest difficulty in finding a room near the other participants, and had had to go some distance from the town centre to a guest house still showing traces of the colonial style, Uhuru

Mansion, a low, white building whose wings were prolonged by a string of attractive little chalets, raised one step above the ground, and overlooking a spongy lawn speckled with little pink flowers, which really had no right to be there.

Every morning, through her bathroom window, Clarence watched the comings and goings of the waiters who carried out to a long table, set up in the the open air, trays of sliced papaw, fleshy mangoes, scrambled eggs and porridge, followed by a procession of steaming coffee-pots. At half past eight a timid little bell signalled to the guests that they could approach, the doors of the chalets all opened simultaneously, people scurried out bare-foot and hungry. But at half past eight Clarence's taxi was already waiting, beckoning to her; with all the traffic jams she would never arrive in time for the first session! She scarcely dared grab a slice of toast, a green banana, as she dashed past . . .

'I had landed on the runway of Paradise, but for an ordinary technical stopover.' Such was her frustration that, before she had even left the place, she insisted on making a reservation for the last week of the year, and had paid a deposit, thereby making any change of plans a very costly exercise.

The idea delighted me. With, however, a pang at the idea of leaving Beatrice for the holiday season. If it had only depended on me, I would have willingly included her in the trip, but I know I'm unreasonable when it is a question of her. Clarence would merely have laughed. In her vocabulary, there was 'you two', that is, my daughter and I, and 'we two', man and woman; that we could burden ourselves with the intruder was quite clearly out of the question.

*

In my life so far, Africa, so full of garish colour, had only been a picture, one of those you think you have once glimpsed and forgotten, but which surface in the dark hours, to bring both hope and disturbance.

What did I see of Africa? Very little: the irrepressible market-women at the foot of self-conscious skyscrapers, hordes of children occupying the streets, low walls, pylons, waste lands, and the eyes of the women who shuffle slowly away with a smile and a flicker of their eyelids, women to whom time means nothing.

Is it not a paradox of our civilization that, while we have mastered space, we have become the slave of time? In Africa, you feel less master of the one and less the slave of the other. That is, if you can manage to escape from yourself. I had a try. Uhuro Mansion was, I know, neither deepest Africa nor even the genuine Naïputo, we were just a few Whites and a few Blacks sharing the fruits of a generous earth; but it was the breath of fresh air needed for my sedentary soul.

What Clarence had not told me – a pardonable journalistic peccadillo – was that she had not come just for the calm, the lawns and the papaws with lemon. She also had a 'spot of confirmation' to do, she admitted on the third day, as we were driving along in a hired car, with me at the wheel, in the right-hand seat, English fashion, while she held maps and guide-books. Didn't we feel like a trip to the Equator, if only to step on the boundary mark that denotes it? It was two hours drive from Naïputo; on the way we could make a detour, just a little out of our way, along the river Nataval.

Those who have read the history of the first years of the

new century will have understood: it was on the banks of the Nataval that the first acts of violence were said to have erupted, linked to the matter which concerns us. Some villagers accused the authorities of distributing 'Indian beans' – that was how they were known in East Africa – in the territory of certain ethnic groups, with the intention of diminishing their reproductive capacity and so, in the long run, decimating them. A health centre was ransacked, about thirty people were hurt, including four European tourists who happened to be passing, and it was thanks to their misadventure that the world got wind of these incidents, which were, on the whole, insignificant.

Clarence was keen to see the damaged health centre with her own eyes and to talk to the villagers. In two minutes our car was surrounded by a crowd shouting and yelling, not at us personally, but simply a chorus of recriminations, some in English, others in Swahili. Two policemen arrived, afraid that our presence might provoke more troubles, and asked us to leave. I didn't have to be asked twice. This episode didn't exactly fit in with my idea of a holiday. However, I refrained from lecturing my companion. She was one of those people who feel guilty and useless as soon as they stop working; this little walk-about put her conscience at ease for the rest of the trip.

It also provided her with some evidence which she would find useful. For soon more riots broke out, in Sri Lanka, Burundi, South Africa, triggered off by similar allegations. It has never been established, to the best of my knowledge, that the methods of selective births were used deliberately at that time as an instrument of discrimination against racial, ethnic or religious groups. But this was said repeatedly, and the suspicion spread.

Everyone is aware that in every country delicate balances exist, which have to be preserved. It would not surprise me if some ruler or other had had the idea of distributing the 'beans' among ethnic groups which were traditionally hostile to him, while preserving the demographic growth of his own people. One day, no doubt, researchers will establish the facts, which will only be of interest to a handful of historians. Facts are of less importance than the attitudes they engender, and as far as these were concerned, we were going to witness year after year, wave after wave of accusations, recriminations, widespread hatred.

Especially in rural areas. Inhabitants of towns do not know each other so well, do not know their numbers. In a village, if over the years one notes a drastic fall in the number of girls, the old people, both men and women, become uneasy. They are the ultimate repository of the instinct for survival. Feeling their community threatened, they denounce the curse on them, they grumble, band together, look for those responsible: have the men been 'doped'? are their wives in league with them? what about the health centre? the rival ethnic group? the authorities? and why not the former colonizer? Doesn't the criminal invention come from him?

I won't claim that, when we visited the banks of the Nataval, my companion and I were aware of the abyss towards which this universal suspicion was hurtling us, this jungle of hostilities in which everyone felt himself a victim and saw nothing but predators around him. The ransacking of a village health centre could not, by any criterion, constitute a remarkable event. There were probably thousands of similar incidents throughout the world, in which neither the number, nor the fame of the victims justified any mention. Only the governments concerned sometimes grew anxious.

A few people in authority were far-sighted enough, quite early on, to denounce the 'substance', its inventors and manufacturers, and to warn their public against this scourge. But their voices remained muffled. Most rulers merely forbade any future publication of statistics listing births by sex, ethnic group, region or religion. Even global population statistics became confidential, and those which were published were, as a general rule, drastically adjusted. Demographers tore their hair, talked of 'unimaginable decline' in the collection of data, a hundred-years-backward leap; yet this became the norm, very soon people grew used to tables dotted with 'figures not available', 'no data', 'approximate calculation' and other admissions of ignorance.

It must be recognized, moreover, that the method proved efficacious. Less and less was heard of those village outbreaks of anger. We know nowadays that they were frequent, violent, and not always contained. They aroused, in any case, less of a stir in those years than the controversies which began to agitate the countries of the North.

M

The very next day after my return from Africa, a short note in an unfamiliar handwriting informed me that Vallauris had just died. Paris was covered in snow. My godfather had ventured out into his street for a stroll. He had felt unwell and collapsed.

It was a very private funeral. Clarence wished to accompany me; Irene and Emmanuel Liev were also there, three of Vallauris's colleagues and a quite young woman, whom none of us seemed to know, but who clearly appeared in the role of the widow. With no weeping, no widow's weeds; her way of raging against death was to be beautiful, the most beautiful, the most elegant, to testify that André had known how to love life to the end, and that life had loved him.

In view of her age, probably nearing forty, she could only have been a kid when my godfather was already enjoining me: 'Confine yourself to the noblest form of promiscuity: that means never making love unless you're in love; and without considering marriage.' There was not the slightest doubt that the 'widow' had entered his life after a string of other loves; however she had the melancholy privilege of being his last companion. Had she been living with him? Was she hiding in some remote room on those Sundays when I came to visit him? Or did she hurry away before our appointed meeting?

Be that as it may, it was her hand that I was the first to shake at the end of the service; all the others queued up behind me to do the same. She submitted to this unexpected ritual with an imperceptible grimace of amusement; perhaps she was thinking of André's smile if he could view the scene.

Of us all, the most moved was Emmanuel, whose wife glanced anxiously at him. To see 'junior' die made him more aware of the arrhythmia of his own heart and the creaking of his bones.

I walked a short distance with him towards the cars.

'That little rotter Vallauris, going for a walk in the snow, when he can't stand the cold!'

He was furious with him. I made some platitudinous reply about fate, the weather, the inevitable.

I had just taken leave of the Lievs, when the 'widow' caught up with me.

'I found this envelope intended for you on André's desk.'

I let Clarence drive so that I could read the letter in the car. It was not a last will and testament, only my friend's demise conferred on it a comparable solemnity. The envelope bore my name and address, and was already stamped. The contents simply said: 'I have an idea that I'd like to discuss with you at our next meeting; I'm putting it to you now to give you time to think it over, to get to work on it, perhaps we can consolidate it without too much delay.

'Here it is: it seems to me that the time is ripe for the formation of a group which I would call, provisionally, the "Network of Sages", which would cover a great many countries and whose role would be to alert public opinion and the different authorities to the dangers arising from the irresponsible manipulation of the human species. I am revolted by the way this phenomenon has become standard practice, and by my compatriots' indifference, indifference all the more incomprehensible in that the danger is not limited to the countries in the South; it would be as misleading as it is criminal to preach or to tolerate a miraculous, final solution to our problems by the loathsome expedient of rampant genocide.

'I thought of Liev as chairman of the "Network", and you and your companion as joint secretaries, thus ensuring efficient administration.

'I have a few more ideas about this matter that we can talk about when you next visit me.'

This last sentence reminded me of the seventy-five or so Sundays that 'our conversation' had lasted. He had brought me a priceless stock of knowledge and experiences, I owed it to his memory to pick up enthusiastically the idea which had fallen from his hands. That same evening I phoned Liev, not doubting for one moment what his reply would be. He shared André's concern and was as anxious as me to pay tribute to him in this way.

But did he not think the title 'Network of Sages' somewhat pompous, a trifle ridiculous?

'Not at all,' he flashed back. 'Wisdom is the forgotten virtue of our times. A scientist who is not also a wise man is either dangerous or, at the best, useless. And then the word "Network" has an aura of mystery, ambiguity, something a bit provocative which will excite people's curiosity. No, André was right, the "Network of Sages" is a good name. I'm for it!'

Clarence had reacted with the same enthusiasm, so we

decided to publish the following boxed insert in four newspapers with an international readership:

'We, the undersigned, being men and women involved in science, the media, culture and action, anxious to spare our common Earth the suicidal enterprises which could once again unleash hatred and distort progress, call for the creation of a "Network of Sages" who would strive for the following aims:

– to put an end to all manipulation of the human species, in particular by means of those iniquitous inventions which involve discrimination by sex, race, ethnic group, religion, or according to any other criterion;

– to promote, by every means, a rapid closure of the gap dividing the North from the South of the planet;

– to persevere in alerting public opinion and warning the authorities against the rise of hatred and intolerance.'

There followed a list of 'sponsors', whom Liev and Clarence had already sounded out, as well as an address – mine, rue Geoffroy-Saint-Hilaire – to which signatures and contributions towards the cost of publishing the appeal could be sent.

The thirty odd 'sponsors' were listed in alphabetical order with the sole exception of André Vallauris who, in spite of his initial V, figured first with, in brackets, a discreet 'In Memoriam'.

When, a few days later, I looked at the published text, boxed in with a shaded surround which made it stand out, I was proud of having made my friend this posthumous gift, but at the same time embarrassed to see my name and address displayed in this way to millions of potential readers. What a disappointment if I only received a handful of messages of support! What a job if I received ten thousand!

When would I manage to read them? How would I answer them all?

I wouldn't like you to imagine that, submerged in these trivial considerations, I neglected the essential, the contents, Vallauris's, Liev's and Clarence's battle, of which I was now in the front line. But it is a fact that I had made my entrance, as it were, with extreme apprehension, which I never lost. I am anxious to make this clear, here and now, so that there is no misunderstanding about my subsequent behaviour.

In the weeks following the publication of the insert, Liev phoned me every morning. He invariably began by apologizing for interrupting my shower or my breakfast, before enquiring in detail about that day's mail. I counted out the number of letters for him, about twenty on an average, the ideal figure for me, since it indicated a sustained interest without crushing me beneath the load.

Emmanuel, whom I jokingly addressed as 'Mr Chairman', was like a cat on hot bricks at the other end of the line while I opened envelope after envelope as fast as I could. This one was from my colleague Favre-Ponti, apparently bearing no ill-will; one from a member of the Academy, others from a former minister, a rabbi, a biologist; the most unexpected letter bore the signature of a Chicago lawyer who had known Vallauris well, and even worked for three years with his law-chambers. His name was Don Gershwin, of the firm of Gershwin and Gershwin, 'Attorneys-at-law'.

The first part of his letter was devoted to our mutual friend, of whose death he had only just learned. He recalled in particular the words with which André had greeted him when he first turned up at his chambers: 'I always trust an Anglo-Saxon who loves Paris. Even if he is a lawyer!'

However, it was the second part of the letter which was important. While giving his unreserved approval to the initiative of the 'Network of Sages', Gershwin begged me to supply him, as quickly as possible, with the documents in my possession concerning the 'substance', its medical, social and other effects, 'in view of a trial which could well prove to be a test case'.

André had more than once pointed out to me that in France theoretical discussions tended to turn indefinitely on moral or political principles, whereas, in the United States, they began and ended in front of a judge; in his capacity as a lawyer, he longed somewhat for such a situation.

Under the circumstances, I think that the 'Network' would have long remained a pious letterbox, if it had not been for the Chicago 'test case'; followed, it is true, by the all too celebrated 'Vitsiya' affair.

N

For many people nowadays the name of Don Gershwin doesn't mean anything; only that of Amy Random sticks in their minds. She was the young wife of an Illinois farmer and had wanted her first child to be the boy her husband desired. Stupidly, but in all innocence, simply with the naïve wish to have Harry give her a big kiss and then proudly pick up his son, she had procured from her chemist certain 'capsules', containing a powder which she had sprinkled on the foam of the beers which she poured for her husband. Whereupon the couple had had a very active sex life and Harry Junior was born the next winter, followed a year later by twins, Ted and Fred. The father was in his seventh heaven, but now he was very keen to have a daughter.

Considerate as ever, Amy went to see her chemist to ask him for the requisite treatment. Alas! he was sorry, the 'reverse' product didn't exist, not yet. So did she have to rely on luck? Alas! the chemist repeated, with the virility that her husband had acquired – those were his exact words – she would have to wait many years to have some chance of giving birth to a girl.

Scientists quite obviously suspected the well-nigh irreversible character of the 'substance', especially when administered in strong doses; but no one had taken the trouble to point this out to Amy, nor to the millions of other users.

Furious, desperate, consumed with guilt, she finally overcame her fear and revealed all to Harry. For several days he accused her of every kind of sorcery, of black magic, threatening to beat her black and blue and throw her off the farm. But he was not really a violent man and Amy, a plumpish redhead with a freckled nose, and wide astonished eyes, had the knack of getting round him. Soon they were making their way, hand in hand, to consult their lawyer, who, aware that he was more competent in litigation between banks and farmers than in medical disputes, advised them to consult the Chicago firm of Gershwin and Gershwin.

The couple threatened to see their local chemist hanged. Don Gershwin persuaded them to lay the blame directly at the manufacturers' door.

The Amy Random affair was to be, in a way, the action against the 'substance', and a turning point in public opinion and the attitude of the authorities.

The danger was that the old and often violent quarrel between 'Pro-life' and 'Pro-choice' would be given new impetus; Don Gershwin was able to avoid this. He skilfully managed to attract into his camp both the enemies of abortion and the most ardent defenders of women's rights; to the latter he pointed out that the product sold to his client was an odious instrument of discrimination, since it gave only boys the right to be born. He was also supported by the Churches, as well as by those in scientific and medical circles, where the methods practised by Dr Foulbot and his North American imitators were regarded with suspicion and contempt.

What is more, the lawyer was able to win over to his cause

the mass of public opinion, by showing that the manufacturers had abused the confidence of the users, since they
had hidden from them the practically irreversible character
of the treatment; I think that it was in the course of the trial,
and the vast debate which surrounded it, that the barbaric
term 'gynosterilization' was used for the first time, and even,
more pithily but, I have to admit, equally incorrectly, just
'sterilization', to characterize the effects of the 'substance'.

The Amy Random affair was the talking point of America
for nearly two years in fact, and it ended with the responsible
manufacturer having to pay two million dollars compensation to the couple. It was not an enormous sum compared
with damages awarded in other so-called 'medical' disputes;
but when you realize that several hundred thousand similar
actions were to be brought that same year, on the same
grounds, and with equal chance of obtaining satisfaction, you
can understand the extent of the catastrophe for the
manufacturers. All those who had gone in for this traffic
went bankrupt; some ended up in prison; others preferred to
leave the country.

Over and above the judicial and financial aspects of the
Random affair, it was to be a salutary eye-opener for all
Northern countries. Up to Beatrice's fifth year – I hope no
one will mind my dating events from my daughter's birth; I
have my reasons, which indulgent readers will not fail to
spot; and besides Beatrice was more or less born with the
century, and any cavilling historian only needs to make a
minute adjustment – so, as I was saying, up to the fifth year
after Beatrice, the countries in the North had watched from
the sidelines as the evil spread. They were merely onlookers,

at times turning a blind eye, at times suspicious, and for the most part indifferent – that was the normal range of people's attitudes whenever it was a question of 'down South'. And the 'substance' was indeed, in everyone's eyes, something from 'down South'. Or, to put it crudely, in the language of many people at the time, something that only' concerned under-developed peoples.

Had not the North resolved its population problems? It had attained the desirable negative growth, with no surplus, no superfluity; what is more, opinion polls showed clearly that couples here had no preference between boys and girls. No disproportion to be feared. The whole business could be discussed at leisure, like so many other things, everything would remain purely theoretical, nothing affecting them physically. I am not being ironical, or not very. I am trying to reproduce what was being thought at the time. Not exactly in my immediate circle. Not by Liev. Not by Clarence. But that was the general opinion.

It is true that in the industrialized world, the 'substance' remained for a long time unknown, or almost. When some people did get wind of it, they associated it with some quack remedy. It was the United Nations report, and the ensuing discussion, in the year of Beatrice's birth, which para-doxically first gave some scientific credibility to Dr Foulbolt's process. So, it was the fruit of long labratory research! So, its efficacity was proven!

When drugs containing the 'substance' were put on sale legally in chemists' shops in Paris, London, Berlin or Chicago, people did not queue up to purchase them. But stocks were quietly cleared, replenished, and quickly sold out again. Who were the customers? In Europe there was no shortage of investigators, quick off the mark, to shout from the rooftops that the purchasers were for the most part Turks, Africans, North Africans; and, in the United States, Hispanics. They were not really Northerners, it was said reassuringly, just those who had chosen to live there, bringing their 'tropical mentalities' with them.

For a long time, people refused to admit that every day more and more local men and women had joined this dark-skinned horde. Only 'dropouts', of course, 'down-and-outs', 'misfits', 'mavericks', or to quote a most learned study published at the time, 'the last upholders of archaic mentalities'; and when the case of Amy Random was first brought up, certain sections of the press did not hesitate to call her 'an illiterate farmer's wife', 'a housewife who was being used as a pawn and whom publicity would make choke on her own broom'.

I said 'certain sections of the press'; if Clarence were writing these lines, she would be much harder on her colleagues. At the time, she got the impression that the whole of the media did nothing but transmit, in a thousand different ways, the same misleading message, namely that the North had nothing to fear, that the incidence of the 'substance' was 'negligible', 'insignificant', 'extremely limited', 'reduced', 'residual', 'under control' . . . For a short time she amused herself collecting all these more or less synonymous expressions; she had counted twenty-four, I think, or twenty-seven, when one day this little game ceased to seem amusing.

'You sometimes imagine that with so many newspapers, radios, TV channels, you're going to hear an infinite number of different opinions. Then you discover it's just the opposite: the power of these means of communication only amplifies the dominant opinion of the time, to the point when it becomes impossible to hear any other bell ringing.'

I shrugged.

'Your colleagues only reflect . . .'

'That's just it! The media reflects what people say, people reflect what the media says. Aren't people ever going to tire of all these soul-destroying effects of distorting mirrors?'

Without even getting up, she punctuated her words with the action of a footballer, venting his disappointment.

'Oh, to give all that a good kick!'

I have to say that her indignation had been roused by a most 'reassuring' opinion poll published that very day. It had been carried out by a Frankfurt magazine in five German *Länder*, and revealed that, out of a hundred couples wanting a child, sixteen preferred a boy, sixteen would rather have a girl, while sixty-eight per cent didn't mind which sex.

'A wonderful balance, so scrupulously symmetrical,' Clarence commented in an article that created a great stir at the time. 'What an eloquent demonstration of the decline of misogyny! These results correspond, moreover, to what we already know of the current thinking about this matter in the whole of Northern Europe.

'The problem,' she added, 'is that the existence of this damnable "substance" contaminates everything with its poison. Ever since it's become widely distributed, ever since it's become available in every town and village, ever since eminent personalities have conferred legitimacy and respectability on this method, figures no longer have the same meaning.

'The calculation implied by these new facts is alas! very simple. The truth is, out of the sixty-eight couples who don't mind what sex their future child is, thirty-five are bound to have boys, and thirty-three will have girls, based on normal demographic probabilities; out of the sixteen who want a girl, there would be a similar distribution, let us say, in round figures, eight per cent; on the other hand, out of the sixteen couples who want a boy, there could well be sixteen male births. So, if we add those up: out of one hundred new-born babies, fifty-nine boys against forty-one girls!'

Clarence had not done any special research; she had simply looked at the figures with her usual mixture of common sense and sixth sense. Nevertheless her prognosis was to be proved astonishingly accurate; in fact, it is estimated that, at the time when the 'substance' was being most widely distributed, one girl in eight, perhaps even one in seven, 'failed to be born' in Germany. And, in a country where there was already anxiety about the low fertility, and even a steady decline in the birth rate among the indigenous population, this phenomenon was to become daily a little more traumatic, and even an obsession.

I need not emphasize that Northern Europe was reckoned, at the time of the survey, to be one of the least 'macho' regions on the planet Earth; the birth of a girl was welcomed as warmly as that of a boy. Nevertheless, even there, the ravages of the curse could be considerable.

It is easier to understand at present the confusion which took hold of the authorities and public opinion when certain statistics concerning the birth rate in Southern and Eastern Europe were disclosed.

I would not like to burden these memoirs with figures which it would be easy to find in reference books; to those interested in such data, I recommend reading the brochure published in the year Seven by the European authorities in Brussels, under the half poetic, half apocalyptic title, which produced its effect: '. . . *and depopulation everywhere*'.

By great fortune, there is not everywhere depopulation. But what a heavy price we are still paying!

0

Round about Beatrice's eighth birthday, I chose to stop all my teaching and research temporarily, the Museum having granted me indefinite paid leave. This was quite exceptional, but everyone was now conscious of living under exceptional conditions. The key word was 'rescue', and because the 'Network of Sages' had been the first of the Cassandras, it seemed like a possible life-line.

Before enlarging on the role which I found myself playing, I ought perhaps to give a slightly better description of the prevailing climate, for those who did not live through this period.

I have referred briefly to the disputes which were troubling Europe and the United States; I have only made passing mention of the first outbreaks of violence in the Third World. I must here add some details which seem to me essential to the understanding of what is to follow.

First of all, rows over the 'substance' and the collective methods of 'selective birth rate', 'discriminatory abortion', 'sterilization' were becoming a daily global phenomenon. True, the inventors and manufacturers were being charged, but the fact that these heads rolled – quite legitimately, moreover – no longer sufficed. In the North, the authorities were accused of negligence, lacking in foresight, being in some way in collusion. In the South, as I have said, the quarrels were between different ethnic groups, different communities; there were also attacks – often unjust – on the medical profession as well as the authorities; then, increasingly, the former colonial power, and more simply the Westerner, came to be referred to as the guilty parties, the source of all the evil. Was not the diabolical invention conceived in the West? Was it not the Westerner who sought in this way to 'sterilize' the masses of human beings who differed from him in colour, religion or amount of wealth? Simplistic, absurd accusation for anyone who has followed the affair from start to finish. But such was the insidious character of the 'substance' that a population could never decide with any certainty if they had been sterilized by the malicious action of an enemy or by the fault of their own ancestral traditions.

Iniquitous, Foulbot's invention? I am the first to agree. But no less iniquitous was the outlook of those who encouraged hundreds of millions of men and women to have recourse to such a treatment. Moreover, it was the confrontation of the iniquities of modernism with those of archaism which gave the events I witnessed such importance.

Very few people at the time expressed the argument in these terms, but everyone felt the inexorable increase in tension. It would be tedious to enumerate the riots, assassinations, kidnappings, hijacks, ransackings; I simply want to say here that henceforth this universal reality, of vague but menacing proportions, was present in people's minds; that many guessed, moreover, the extent of the ravages already caused by the 'substance' in various lands, even if it became more difficult than ever to produce figures to substantiate these; however, when, in the North, there was talk of 'rescue' it was in the first place a question of rescuing the North.

Of two dangers, one immense but distant and vague, the other less deadly but close at hand, is it not human to give priority to the second?

It is easy today to rant and rail. It is easy to prove, with hindsight, that the North, by allowing the disaster in the South to grow, compromised its own prosperity and safety, and the South, by attacking the North, condemned itself to decline. Everyone, at the time, wanted to avoid the most immediate dangers as quickly and cheaply as possible.

I leave to others, who have more years ahead of them, the job of weighing up the pros and cons. For my part, I have always admitted that these questions were beyond me; I could, at best, point out the problem, since Vallauris had bequeathed me a certain amount of lucidity; but no one should be taken in by the pretentious title 'Network of Sages'. By what miracle could we have prevented the calamities? What were we, except a helpless association of people desirous of a different future? What else did we do but talk, write, talk, like preachers droning on endlessly for an interminable Sunday?

However, those who knew this period cannot have forgotten that sublime old man, Emmanuel Liev, with his huge schnozzle, his bat-wing ears, and especially his voice which spoke to all and also spoke to each individually. He had become a sort of 'universal grandfather', reassuring even when his intention was to scare.

Difficult for me to evaluate objectively the part he or the Network played; I like to think they were not insignificant. It is true it needed a whole concatenation of events – lawsuits, outbreaks of violence, alarming statistics – before people began to wake up finally to the urgency of the situation in Europe and the whole of the North. But I am not taking excessive liberties with the facts when I state that most of the decisions taken by the authorities at the time had been inspired by members of our group.

By speaking more specifically of Liev, I wanted to draw attention to the person who was, up till his death, our standard-bearer, our fetish. But there were many of us, at first dozens then hundreds, too scattered throughout the world for us all to know each other, too concerned with efficacity to organize chaotic general meetings. No, we kept to our idea of a 'network', a sort of invisible thread linked us, implicit ideals united us, and we were kept on the alert by the sense of urgency which we all felt.

Some of our ideas were, as I said, accepted and put into practice, others were the object of controversy; others again were to prove ineffectual, although resulting from the best intentions. The common aim of all these suggestions was to incite the population to have girls in sufficient numbers to restore the balance of births, and to return to the fertility rate of before the crisis. It must be understood that in the 'leanest' years an estimated million girls 'failed to be born' in the whole of the continent of Europe; nothing compared to the 'guestimate' for certain lands in the South; but sufficient to justify the fear of depopulation.

It was necessary, in the first place, to prevent fresh people from using the 'substance'; that was the least of the problems. It was forbidden to manufacture or market any products 'responsible for discriminatory birth rates' and even if there were some sales under the counter, their distribution in most countries in the North was negligible from now on. But that was no longer enough. In view of the impressive number of men already treated – perhaps one should say 'contaminated' – the deficit in female births would continue for several years to come, so exacerbating the imbalance. Therefore the tendency had to be reversed, by various means.

On the scientific and technological level, there was an attempt to speed up the manufacture of the substance favouring the birth of girls, commonly called the 'reverse substance'; research was already well advanced, there already existed a prototype, but distribution was finally abandoned because of certain side effects which had been observed and which the researchers had never been able to eliminate. Moreover this project was much contested. Even within the Network, those who were opposed on principle to any genetic manipulation, thought it illogical to combat one evil by another, encouraging one distortion to compensate for the ravages of another. On the other hand, the allocation of funds for the production of an 'antidote', that is, a treatment able to reduce the action of the 'substance' in those who had already used it, or even totally nullify its effects, was unanimously applauded by everyone; however, the research progressed more slowly than anticipated, and even when it was successful, the method proved complicated, costly, therefore difficult to use on a large scale.

Certainly, the most efficacious measures, the ones which contributed the most decisively to re-establishing the balance of births, were of a monetary nature: governments, one after another, decided to grant important tax rebates on the birth of a daughter to families with a high income, to be continued throughout her childhood and adolescence; for families on low incomes it was decided to grant special child benefits, sufficiently substantial for many women to be tempted to stop work in order to have a child – ideally, a girl.

Several countries, alas! thought good to extend these advantages to families that adopted a little girl, for whom adoption formalities were simplified. In vain did the Network denounce this measure, whose pernicious nature should have immediately struck everyone: in a world where girls were becoming rare, where their 'acquisition' offered financial benefits, an uncontrollable, sordid traffic was soon organized, stirring up hatred between rich and poor countries, of which I shall soon have occasion to speak.

Other measures, better inspired, also had their effect, in particular, a publicity campaign on the large and small screens, and on giant posters; they showed a man lifting up above his head a little girl on whom he gazed adoringly; and underneath, a laconic slogan: 'A father, a daughter.'

The man on the hoardings was me, and the girl, naturally, was Beatrice. It was the adman who suggested I parade myself in this way, but I suspect he was prompted by Clarence. At first I laughed at the idea; then, in the end, I agreed, in a moment of mental aberration, letting myself be persuaded that if sincerity could do the trick then the way I looked at Beatrice would be convincing.

It wasn't easy for me to lift up a little girl of nine, already big for her age, and to hold her above my head for several heavy seconds; however the photographer managed to give the picture an impression of movement in flight which suggested creation, play, and one generation rising after another.

As long as I was still in the studio – hundreds of shots over three days had been necessary – the idea had remained an idea. But when I saw myself more than lifesize on walls, I felt as if I were crushed; my first thought was of the Museum; fortunately, I thought, I'm not going there any more, I'd never be able to stand the students' laughter or my colleagues' banter.

But this anecdotal aspect is of little importance, the idea of the campaign went further than a poster and a slogan. It was a question of getting it into people's heads that a daughter-and-heir was as valuable as a son-and-heir. Legislation had already progressed in that direction, save in one respect, a formality but still a fundamental question: that of surnames.

How could this be solved? By giving the child the double surname of the father and mother, as in Spain for example? Clearly, that would not do away with male chauvinism or, according to a term used in debates at the time, 'male heirism'. So what was to be done? To give every child the choice, on his or her majority, between the father's or mother's patronymic?

For my part, I was for a more radical reform: the imposition of the matronymic. Just as it had long been obligatory for children to be known by the father's surname, henceforth it would be equally obligatory for them to bear that of the mother. I shall not repeat all my arguments here, but simply indicate that the basic idea was the radical reversal of the notion of heredity to bring it more into line with biological logic and more favourable to the perpetuation of the species.

If my proposal was not followed through in its entirety, many countries did agree to modifying their legislation on surnames; the word 'patronymic' is no longer pronounced with the same assurance as formerly.

But my ideas and my contribution are of little import; I have no pride of authorship on this subject. The only thing that deserves to be pointed out, concerning those years, is that the sequence of measures adopted in the North seemed to be effective. Female births gradually increased. And, to the relief of one and all, it was soon announced, supported by statistics, that depopulation had been halted.

It was probably for this reason that it was not immediately realized that the harm had already been done.

P

Amid the deafening chorus of self-satisfaction heard in all the countries in the North, a few voices were nevertheless raised, even at that time, to ask the only real question: what, in the coming years, would be the consequences of the recent serious imbalance of births? They were only listened to with half an ear, as a man just saved from drowning might listen to someone telling him not to sit in a draught in his wet clothes.

And if this rescued man were told that a stranger was still drowning at the other end of the beach, would he have rushed to save him? No, he would have lain there, motionless, exhausted, not able to believe his luck, continually dwelling on his moments of terror, panic and final rescue. That is how I explain the initial failure of the campaign launched by the Network in the year Thirteen, with the slogan, 'The North is saved, let us save the South.'

Even today, I can scarcely believe what I read or heard. The same old arguments, those used by Pradent, were dished up verbatim, as if they had merely been justified by the events. The North was threatened with depopulation, they said, a rescue operation was needed; as far as the South was concerned, on the other hand, everyone knows it is over-populated, a decline in the fertility rate would not be a distortion there but, on the contrary, a beneficial re-adjustment of the balance. What is more, now that 'our countries' had experienced a decrease in population, at least an equivalent reduction 'down South' was becoming all the more desirable. To achieve this end, all means were good . . .

And there was I, thinking the old demons had been buried! Hearing these arguments, I remembered a discussion I had had with André. At the time I was twelve or thirteen, and he had asked me, out of the blue, 'Do you believe in ghosts?' 'No!' I had protested, hurt that he could have thought me receptive to such nonsense. 'Well, you're wrong,' he retorted. 'I'm not talking about corpses which haunt grave-yards at night and grab you with their claws. I'm talking about ghost-ideas with claws which come back to haunt you, and which are just as blood-thirsty: you'll meet them at every stage of your life, and you'll never be able to kill them off because they are already dead.' Allegory or not, my adolescent mind was long haunted by these ghost-ideas; even today I can still see some of them, I hunt them down vehemently everywhere, albeit without illusions.

This was more or less my frame of mind when the wretched business, which came to be known as the 'Vitsiya' or 'Celestial Ark' affair blew up. An event as tragic as it was farcical, and just to recall it covers me with shame, as it ought to cover all my contemporaries with shame. But what can you do, that was the state the world had got into!

I have already had occasion to mention that many governments had decided to facilitate the adoption of girls abroad, so as to make up for the deficit in female births, and that the Network had protested in vain. It was our opinion that adoption can certainly act as emotional compensation, but under no circumstances should it be used for demo-graphic compensation; we felt it represents a wonderful human commitment, on condition that it remain strictly individual; that it should never become the object of any commercial negotiation, nor involve any financial benefits. When it is a question of children, a very fine line separates the sublime from the sordid, the generous from the criminal . . .

But the authorities, like the public, having learned their lesson with the fear of depopulation, couldn't be bothered with such nice distinctions. They thought in terms of rates, deficits, global stability, and were quite ready to see a legitimate, even beneficial action in the massive transfer of girls from the South to the North.

Encouraged by legislation, as much as by popular sentiment, an American 'televangelist' of Ukrainian origin, whose real name escapes me now, but who was commonly known as 'Vitsiya' – which I think means 'father' in the Ukrainian dialect – decided to launch an immense operation whose aim was to transport to the North ten thousand new-born infants, nearly all girls, from Brazil, the Philippines, Egypt, and several other countries in the South. Accompanied by enormous publicity, he organized a huge air-lift, which he pompously christened, the 'Celestial Ark'.

You have to have lived through those days personally, or experienced this 'real life spectacle', as some people liked to say in those days, to grasp the whole significance of what happened. Several television channels reckoned the Vitsiya's operation was a veritable boon for the media, capable of moving and exciting to the nth degree, a public particularly sensitive to everything which had to do with population problems; and that it was even possibly a question of a great historical event which it would be unforgivable to 'miss'.

So, for forty-eight hours, an entire week-end, hundreds of

millions of households remained glued to their TV sets, watching the pictures of the operation repeated over and over again, interspersed with interviews with the hero of the day, a giant with a shining beard and bushy, fair eyebrows.

The Vitsiya was not a vulgar crank, hungry for publicity, as people today like to depict him. And the argument he developed was not unreasonable. 'Let us take,' he said, 'the case of a girl who has just been born in a Sudanese village. Her expectation of life, in view of the infantile mortality and the risks attached to her own eventual childbearing, is approximately forty years; in Europe, this same girl would live to the age of eighty. Who can decide in cold blood to deprive her of half her life-span?'

A question: should not this child rather be helped in her own country, to allow her a better life in the heart of her own community? The Vitsiya's reply: 'That is exactly what people have been repeating to us for half a century. But nothing has been done. If I don't want this child to die within six months from an epidemic, or be afflicted with some crippling disease, or die in giving birth to her first baby, I cannot wait for all the problems of the planet to be resolved. It is not a matter of studying the fate of one indeterminate individual, one negligible sample fed into some technocrat of a computer. It is a matter of going to the poverty-stricken countries, meeting a child, looking into her eyes and asking oneself, "Am I going to save this child or let her perish?" It's as simple as that. When I know that thousands and thousands of families in the wealthy countries are waiting for this child, ready to welcome her, lavish their love on her, ensure she has the education which will allow her to live her life as a complete human being, to give her a long happy, dignified life, have I the right to hesitate?'

'But in the final resort,' one journalist asked him, 'what are you out to do? To transport all the children of the South to the North?' 'Unfortunately, I can't do that,' the preacher replied with a slightly challenging grin, 'but if I managed to save ten thousand children, my own life would not have been lived in vain.'

Nothing in all these words seemed to me reprehensible or dishonourable. And if the motives behind the operation were not always as noble as he claimed, I am still not convinced, even today, in spite of everything which happened, that the man was a scoundrel. There can be no doubt but that the affair slid horribly out of control, for which he bears the responsibility. But, with the passage of time, the Vitsiya seems merely to have been the noisy agent that revealed the rot to which he scarcely contributed.

If he did err, it was, I think, first and foremost, in the immense scale of his project, and in the incredible blunders associated with this huge scale. So, by insisting on a gigantic operation which could strike the imagination of the public and be a bait to the media, he had deemed it unnecessary to find families in advance to receive all the children, convinced that these would turn up in countless numbers. So he chartered jumbo-jets, bringing to Paris, London, Berlin, Frankfurt, and if my memory is not playing me false, Copenhagen and Amsterdam as well, a first batch of two thousand infants to be 'disposed of' – it's the first expression which occurs to me – and relied on publicity in the media to attract the punters.

In order to dissipate the fears of the potential adoptive parents, he had subjected the children to very meticulous medical examinations, only keeping the healthiest ones. And so that no one could have any doubts about this, he had had posters printed, showing himself carrying an infant on his left arm and brandishing a medical certificate, duly signed, in his right hand. For the occasion he had put on a white hospital coat, probably to look more hygienic, but the poster was unfortunately reminiscent of commercials which had been shown recently, advertising a certain supermarket's sausage department.

This image produced the first negative impression, which was followed by many others. The television channels which covered the event without a break, recorded an unprecedented number of viewers, but the Vitsiya, finding himself on the box at all hours, harassed with questions, exhausted by his trip, gradually let slip some unfortunate expressions. And some even frankly disastrous! Thus he agreed that children who presented the slightest sign of illness, the slightest anomaly, had been turned down. 'So,' it was pointed out to him, 'instead of concern for the ones whose condition justified the most care and attention, you preferred the healthiest, the easiest ones to place.' His explanations were hardly convincing.

In reply to another question, he was heard to explain that he had decided to classify the children in six categories, according to their particular shade of colouring, 'to make it easier for the parents to choose the one who would fit in most harmoniously with their family'; and that, while remaining faithful to the principle of 'one single financial contribution', he would allow a rebate for those who would agree to adopt a child belonging to a different race from their own. There was here a suggestion of one 'purchase price' with a 'sale price' for the surplus stock, which I was not the only person to find nauseating.

The TV stations began to receive calls from outraged

viewers, some even threatening. Then a first incident occurred, when the preacher, praising the countless advantages of transferring the children to the North, had the unfortunate idea of saying that he had taken care to recruit large numbers of infants from Islamic societies, especially Egypt, Turkey, Somalia and Sudan, 'to give them, especially the girls, the means of escaping from the miserable fate which would have awaited them in their own society, and allow them a place in a better religious and cultural environment.' Various Islamic Associations issued press releases protesting, and soon people began to gather, apparently spontaneously, in different districts with large immigrant populations, in France, Holland, Belgium, England, Germany.

On the night of Saturday to Sunday, when Operation 'Celestial Ark' had been going on for nearly twenty-four hours and a new wave of jumbo-jets was expected, riots broke out. In scale, they were reminiscent of the Watts riots in the 1960s and in Los Angeles at the end of the last century; but this time they took place principally in Europe. Probably the Black ghettos of America had too long been eroded by their internal violence. That is one of the explanations which were put forward at the time . . . In any case the only incidents recorded in the United States broke out in Hispanic areas and never reached the extent and fury observed on the Old Continent.

It goes without saying that the tensions had been building up for decades, that the suspicion between the 'nationals' and the immigrant communities was an accepted fact, and everyone had learned to live with it. But, with the exception of occasional, limited, brief flare-ups, violence had remained a hypothetical threat. The 'Celestial Ark' affair, coming after the great fear of depopulation, provoked an outburst. For more than a week, the fury grew, spreading to several dozen European cities, degenerating into uncontrolled riots, admittedly unorganized, but conforming curiously to a sort of model common to such events, with looting and destruction rather than bloodshed; and always attacking the same targets, namely everything which symbolizes either the Government – road signs, police cars, public telephones, buses, official buildings; – or wealth – shops, banks, large cars; or even the medical services.

There were relatively few deaths, a total of about sixty, all countries taken together, but there were no less than eight thousand injured; and, naturally, damage amounting to billions. Towns in Europe were paralysed for a whole week as if by a general strike, streets remaining dark and deserted and often strewn with debris . . .

And long after the week was over, distrust persisted, as if a toxic substance had long been mixed with the air that everyone was breathing.

Q

So it needed this gigantic farce, followed by a continent overwhelmed with fear, to undermine people's inviolable egotism and for the idea of rescue to apply finally to the whole inhabited earth.

The Network of Sages, in a declaration which we tried to make both loud and solemn, demanded the organization, within twelve months, of a world summit on population problems. The idea was timely, it was immediately welcomed enthusiastically. Many heads of state or of government announced their intention of themselves leading their country's delegation.

The headquarters of the United Nations in New York immediately seemed the ideal setting to give the occasion the necessary publicity. It was decided to invite, in addition to governments, certain organizations 'active in the field of humanitarian solidarity', as well as a small number of individuals 'who could give the participants the benefit of their knowledge and their wisdom'.

These words seemed custom-made for Emmanuel Liev's face and voice to be conspicuous in this gathering, or rather, to tower above it.

Once more, but for the last time, he was admirable. With his frail figure, his head dreamed up by some divine caricaturist, he stepped up on to the platform, like a peasant climbing on to a heap of stones, and gazed around at these hundreds of kings, presidents, ministers and other excellencies, like a bird perched aloft, not aloofly, but without deference. I almost expected him to address them as 'Children'. He could have done so; at eighty-eight, he was old enough to be the father of them all.

However, he chose to begin as follows: 'I hope I shall be forgiven for not opening with the usual formalities. I don't know what they are and it is too late for me to learn them. So, I shall just address you by the title, with which every one of you should feel honoured: "Men of goodwill!" '

Emmanuel spoke for nine minutes, without notes but without hesitation, in front of an audience so silent they could have been meditating. His speech was followed live in nearly every country in the world. It still seems to me today, with the passage of time, a model of clarity, and yet for all that, not devoid of hope.

'There are countless numbers of us on this earth,' he said. 'Some will say, too great a number. I do not think so. Neither do I think we should go on multiplying indefinitely; for me this "cradles' revenge", by which subjected peoples sometimes seek to throw off the yoke of dominant minorities, seems pitiful.

'There are countless numbers of us, yes, and no doubt we have multiplied too fast. And yet, if eight billion of our fellow-men drowned in the Mediterranean, do you know by how much the level of the water would rise? By a tenth of a millimeter! Yes, my brothers, my young brothers, we, all the men and women of the six continents, are only a thin layer, a minute layer of flesh and conscience on the face of the earth.

'Do some people speak of congestion? If the Earth is

indeed congested, it is with our greed, our egotism, our exclusions, our so-called "living-space", our "zones of influence" or "safely zones" and also by our futile independences.

'In the course of the last century, our planet was divided between the South with its recriminations and the North with its impatience. Some people became resigned to seeing this as a commonplace cultural or strategic reality. Hatred does not remain indefinitely a commonplace reality. One day, on some pretext or other, an explosion is triggered off and people discover that, for a hundred years, a thousand, two thousand years, nothing has been forgotten, no blow, no fear. Where hatred is concerned, memory is a time-traveller, it feeds on everything, sometimes even on love.

'Few doctrines throughout History have been able to eradicate hatred, most of them have simply tried to deflect it from one object to another: to the infidel, the foreigner, the apostate, the master, the slave, the father. Naturally hatred is only called hatred when we see it in others; the hatred which is in ourselves bears a thousand different names.

'Hatred has today taken the form of a pernicious substance, the fruit of legitimate research, the fruit of this same genetic research which allows us to combat malformations and tumours, the fruit of the same genetic engineering which allows us to improve our food resources. But a pernicious fruit which has brought out the worst instincts in everyone.

'For thousands of years, billions of human beings have lamented the birth of a girl and rejoiced at the birth of a boy. And suddenly there appears a tempter saying to them: "See, your hope can became a reality." For thousands of years, there have been peoples, ethnic groups, races, tribes who have dreamed of destroying those who have committed the unpardonable sin of being different. And then a tempter appears, saying to them: "See, you can decimate them, no one will be any the wiser."

'Sometimes – you will, I am sure, forgive the wild imaginings of an old man – I find myself thinking that the Earthly Paradise mentioned in the Scriptures is not a myth of olden times, but a prophecy, a vision of the future. For several decades men seemed to be in the process of building this Paradise, never before had man been so able to control matter, life, natural energy; he resolved to do away with disease; one day perhaps he would do away with old age, death. My words are not those of an unbeliever; if science has banished the God of "How", it is to make way for the God of "Why". A God who, for his part, will never disappear. I believe him capable of giving man every power, even that of control over life and death, which after all are merely natural phenomena. Yes I believe God capable of associating us, his creatures, with his creation. When I tamper with the genes of a pear-tree, I believe sincerely that God has given me this capacity and this right. But there are forbidden fruit. Not naïvely those of sex or knowledge, as our ancestors believed; the forbidden fruit are more complex, more difficult to define, and it is our wisdom rather than our beliefs which will point them out to us.

'In spite of my white hairs and my supposed wisdom, I admit that I do not know exactly where the frontiers lie which we may not cross. Probably in the direction of the atom, and also certain manipulations of our brain and genes. What I am able to detect with more certainty, if I may say so, are those moments when mankind takes mortal risks with itself, its integrity, its identity, its survival. These are the moments when the noblest of sciences puts itself at the service of the most despicable of aims.

'Events have occurred which give cause for alarm; they are as nothing compared to what is to come. I am carefully weighing every word I utter: certain disasters can no longer be avoided. Let us be aware of this and let us try to avoid the worst.

'There are, throughout the world, thousands of cities, millions of villages, where the number of girls has been regularly declining; in some this phenomenon has lasted for nearly twenty years. I do not intend to speak to you of all those whom a despicable discrimination has prevented from being born. That is no longer the question. I shall tell you in crude terms what I greatly fear, for it is in these terms that the question must be put: I am thinking of the hordes of males who for years will be wandering in search of a non-existent mate; I am thinking of the furious mobs which will form and increase and run amok, driven mad by frustration – not simply sexual, for they will also be deprived of their chance to lead a normal life, to build a family, a home, a future. Can you just imagine the amount of resentment and violence stored up in these people, which nothing will be able to satisfy or appease? What institutions will be able to resist? What laws? What order? What values?

'Yes, violence has already been breaking out all over the place. But this has not yet been the violence of people driven to fury. It has been the violence of worried, anxious people, who have not yet experienced frustration themselves, who have had a family and rejoiced in the birth of a son and heir. They protest, they demonstrate, because they are anxious about the future of their communities, but their anxiety is restrained, since they do not experience the tragedy in their own flesh, since they are in revolt, not against any known evil, but against one that mankind has never yet known, and which remains vague, hypothetical. Tomorrow we shall see the generations of the cataclysm, the generations of men without women, generations amputated of their future, generations whose fury it will be impossible to contain.

'I have had in my hands a confidential report on a big city in the Near East. Today the census shows one and a half million boys under the age of seventeen and less than three hundred thousand girls. I dare not even imagine what the streets of that city will be like in a year's time, in two years, ten years, twenty years . . . Wherever I look, I see violence, madness and chaos.

'For petty, cynical motives, by the diabolical combination of outmoded traditions and corrupt science, the planet which is our home, mankind which is our nation, will traverse the most dangerous zone of upheavals ever seen in our History, and without even the excuse of fate or a plague sent by God.

'Can we still prevent this? We can only try to diminish the consequences. If all possible means were used, if all the nations in the North and South, forgetting their grievances, ignoring their differences, were to mobilize as they would in wartime; if, in the months to come, we began to see a return to a balance between male and female births, if we rid ourselves of our destructive prejudices, if we channelled all frustrated energies towards some gigantic, grandiose, creative, expansive, humanizing work; if we could succeed, without excessive violence, in maintaining some semblance of cohesion and order in the exchanges between the continents, then perhaps this ship which carries us will not capsize. It will be tossed in the storm, it will be damaged, but perhaps we shall avoid shipwreck.'

The speaker stepped forward as if to leave the platform, then returned, thoughtful, troubled, hesitating, to repeat the single word, 'Perhaps.'

When he stepped down from the platform, the reaction was unexpected, unheard-of, to the best of my knowledge unprecedented in the history of the organization. The delegates were stunned for a moment, then began one by one to rise to their feet, but without ovations, without applause. A silent, stricken tribute. And only after Liev had returned to his place, after he had sat down, after he had motioned to his immediate neighbours to sit, only then did the audience resume their seats, which they suddenly found uncomfortable, unsteady.

Emmanuel closed his eyes for a long moment, as if to avoid people's attention. The man on the left was an American member of the Network, Professor Jim Cristobal; on his right was none other than Clarence. When the session resumed somehow or other, she leaned towards the 'Old Man' and whispered in his ear, 'This is fame!'

'Fame indeed,' he replied. 'Impotence and fame!'

R

I didn't go to New York myself. The Network was already sufficiently represented by Liev and several eminent members of various nationalities; and Clarence, my co-secretary, was much more useful than me on this trip, if only by reason of her contacts with the press. So I had followed the conference from a distance and I had found Emmanuel's performance completely appropriate to the situation, that is to say, sufficiently dramatic to cause the necessary element of shock. The attitude of the assembly especially was staggering, even when seen on television, since the commentator had the good taste or the correct instinct to respect the delegates' silence. It was night-time in Paris and Beatrice sat up to watch with me, nestling at my side.

I am still overcome with emotion when I think of that night. Firstly, because it was the obvious triumph of all that Clarence, André, Emmanuel and I myself had been fighting for, for years. Then, because I was watching the events in the company of the person most dear to me. To express it thus may sound very naïve, but never before had I stayed up all night alone together with my daughter. To be sure, at her birth and during the following months, I had spent many a sleepless night with her ravenous and bawling; I don't count those, that was different, she was just a hungry mouth, a larva; on this occasion, she was a real little woman, a beautiful fourteen-year-old girl. It was three in the morning, we had just shared the same apprehensions, the same enthusiasm, and also, when it was all over, a glass or two of champagne.

I had made up my mind to wait till six in the morning – midnight in New York – before phoning Clarence at her hotel. While we waited, I told Beatrice, for the first time coherently and in chronological order, of the events which were to become the subject of this book. Moreover it was by collecting my memories together that night, by trying to organize them, to present them, if I may say so, logically, that for the first time I had some vague half-formed idea of one day setting down in writing the things that had impinged on my life.

My first plan was to relate to Beatrice, perhaps in a series of letters, or by some other approved literary device, the story of the century which expired with her birth, telling her on what shallows it had gone aground. And, perhaps, outlining the characteristics of her own century.

Speakers, like authors, sometimes know the moment when the sentence takes off, as if one passed from one state of awareness to another. You are carried away, you are transfigured. You don't speak, you let yourself go and listen to yourself speaking. You don't write, you simply support your hand so that it does not betray you, like a mount unaware of the journey which the rider imposes on it.

In the course of that sleepless night in Beatrice's company, I was, for two long hours, that inspired speaker; if some recording device had been switched on, my book would have been written, up to this line, with less hesitation, with scrupulous observance of the facts, more consistent with my character, than that which I strive after painfully at my present advanced age.

Beatrice's expression did not change, she kept her face turned to me with the delicate trust of a sunflower turning towards the sun. Seeing her thus, I did not dare stop, or digress or weaken.

When I reached the account of the meeting in New York, I pointed dramatically to the television screen which had just gone blank, as if to say, by way of conclusion, 'And so it is that . . .'

Beatrice obediently turned to look at the screen which I had indicated, but immediately looked back at me.

'You know, when I meet the man of my life, I'd like him to be just like you.'

I was about to retort, with the most affectionately mocking smile, that all daughters have always said that to their fathers. But as I uttered the first syllable, a rascally tear trickled from my eye, and my lips and cheeks began to tremble.

Kneeling on the sofa, Beatrice wiped away my tears with her sleeve, more playful than was her wont.

'Isn't it a disgrace, a big daddy like you crying like a little girl?'

'Isn't it a disgrace, a little girl saying such things to an old daddy?'

She threw her arms round my neck, like when she was that little girl that I carried to her child-minder, a garland still as brown, scarcely any heavier, and warm and moist and smelling of a child's healthy sweat.

Let those who see incest everywhere interpret this as they please: I wished I could remain like this to the end of time, with the arms of this child of my flesh around me, crushed beneath her weight, her hair falling over my eyes. Why should I brush it aside? What else could I have wished to look at?

We were now both silent, and her breathing grew slower and her clasp slackened. Moving as slowly as possible, so as not to wake her, I slipped one arm under her back, the other under her knees, carried her to her bed and laid her down.

As I straightened myself up, I felt a crick in my back. My wretched fifty-year-old bones. Nevertheless, when I chance today – today especially – to set off the same pain by some injudicious action, I would not dream of complaining. For I remember that sleepless night, Beatrice's little face, her breathing as she slept, that sweet heavy burden which I laid down, and my pain, through the soothing balm of memory, becomes a caress, a tease, a lover's affectionate pinch.

I didn't get through to Clarence until the early hours of the morning, after three attempts. She had just come back from a working dinner, devoted to drawing up the final motion for the conference. Triumphant, but exhausted, she nevertheless had the strength to read me out the main points, which repeated, sometimes word for word, Emmanuel Liev's warnings and, combining tact with urgency, recommended to the participants a series of measures: a strict, global ban on the manufacture and distribution of the offending 'substance' and destruction of existing stocks; unified legislation concerning traffic in children; a generously endowed fund to be set up, to assist those countries unable to cope with the situation by their own means; and above all a vast resounding, world-wide campaign whose aim would be to explain why hatred gets out of control.

I have spoken often enough in the preceding pages – but I have to insist on it again – of the enormity of the latter task.

In this matter it was no longer simply a question of the 'substance', nor of all the events which I have referred to in this book. The problem was much more immeasurable – even this pretentious word is here an insipid euphemism: it was a question of nothing more nor less than appeasing, by a propaganda campaign, all the hatred which, throughout the ages, has set man against man. Is not stating the problem in this way sufficient to reveal the unworldiness, the absurdity of such a task? By what miracle could this aim be realized and bring about conciliation? I discussed this with Clarence that same morning, and many more times in the ensuing weeks.

She claimed, and this had some appearance of logic, that the whole human race was afraid, and felt more than ever before the extent to which the survival of the species was threatened, and that the attitude of all the nations in New York showed clearly that an explosion was possible, in any case it was not unthinkable. Obviously it was not a question of doing away with hatred, she inferred, but of curbing the present fury provoked by the 'substance'. Had there not been in the past a comparable reaction, in the face of the risk of nuclear war, which had effectively allowed the cataclysm to be avoided? What is more, she added, we now have means of communication and persuasion which never previously existed; if they were utilized everywhere, simultaneously, with unfailing determination and unlimited means, the miracle might take place.

She argued passionately, vehemently, with the enthusiasm of one who is fighting for her own survival and that of her family.

'Since no doctrine has succeeded in abolishing hatred, perhaps fear will be a better counsellor! Perhaps this is the only chance we have left!'

'Now you're talking like Emmanuel Liev!'

My words, although harmless, seemed to upset my companion. She remained silent for a few minutes, breathing hard, before remarking in a voice suddenly grown barely audible, 'The tragedy is that Emmanuel talks like me in public but he thinks like you.'

Feeling a little guilty for having thus shattered in a few minutes, and from afar, Clarence's touching enthusiasm, I tried to make amends.

'You know, Emmanuel is like André Vallauris. In their childhood, they lived at such close quarters with hatred that they can now smell it from a distance, a great distance. That is their merit, except that they tend to believe it is always on the return and probably invincible. I have myself been too heavily influenced by André. If I listened to myself, if I yielded to my greatest temptations, I would shut myself up at home cursing the world, predicting floods, and when they happened, I would be torn between pleasure in being right and shame for rejoicing in this way. Go off and fight, Clarence, get worked up, breathe fire, for even if events confirm my doubts, my doubts will still be less noble, less honourable than your most naïve illusions.'

'I love you,' came her reply, from New York to Paris. The same words were echoed from Paris to New York. Then I added, 'And you know you can count on your Sancho Panza to the end!'

In the promise I had just made to my heroine, there was, I must acknowledge today, as much genuine love as genuine duplicity. For, if I was ready to back her to the end, it was no longer in the way I had done up till then. I was anxious to remain at her side, to surround her with every care and attention, to guarantee her – and I say this quite seriously – a comfortable and stimulating resting-place to return to after the battle, in a word, I was prepared to be companion, brother, son and father, and more of a lover than ever. However, a temptation was growing in me, which was to become more and more urgent: the temptation to flee from all public activities and return to my laboratory, my scientific books, my microscope, my beloved insects.

I knew that the moment was ill-chosen, that she would consider such an attitude as a betrayal, a desertion, and she would be right. Nevertheless, that same day, under the impetus of that extreme, obsessive urge which comes from sleepless nights, I decided to phone the Director of the Museum who suggested I drop in to see him.

This action was a bit premature, you will say, especially since I had not made up my mind. I agree. But one should behave with temptations as with rare insects; if you come across them, even if you are looking for something else, you must find time to capture them, index them, give them a scientific name, even if you then leave them in a drawer for ten years and forget about them.

So I went round to the Museum, simply to tell the Director, a long-standing colleague, that I didn't rule out a return one day to my laboratory, and to hear him say that if and when I wanted to 'come home' there would always be a place for me and under my own conditions. We made a date, if I may say so, without fixing a date. That was exactly what I wanted.

As I left his office, I suddenly felt overwhelmed with excitement and bliss; rather than cross the road immediately and make my way home, I tramped briskly round the

Botanical Gardens, with my hands clasped behind my back, gazing into the distance. And with every step, the temptation grew stronger, firmly imbedded within me like evidence long suppressed. How could I run counter to my nature in this way? involve myself in this public life which I had always found tyrannical and contemptible? Whether seated in front of my microscope, or facing life, I always wanted to be the observer and not the dissected. By what unconscious perversion had I been able to change places with the insect? What inexplicable excess had caused me to strut about, making an exhibition of myself?

The longer I tramped up and down the paths and the faster I walked, the more my anger, together with euphoria about the future, increased. At the first opportunity I would talk to Clarence, to Emmanuel, then I would begin my metamorphosis without delay, I would change my appearance, grow a bushy grey beard, bushy as befits a scientist determined to be just that, grey as befits a quinquagenarian. So, for a time, no one except my intimate friends would recognize me. I have always found it a problem having to put up with people's gaze. It's not fear of crowds. I can endure being in a congested place, swarming with people, as long as I'm anonymous; but to enter a restaurant, for example, where one individual, just one, may possibly recognize me, is unbearable. I leave at once, suffering physically.

How had I been able to teach, you will ask? I will confess the trick to which I had recourse to get round my phobia: I always arrived for the lecture before my students, I entered an empty classroom, took up my position, spread out my notes, settled into my chair, lost in thought. Then nothing could upset me. But when I had to enter a lecture theatre, walk down the aisle with everyone's eyes upon me, climb on to the platform, every step was a torture, I would have given ten days of my life to be somewhere else. And once I was seated, it took me several minutes to get my breath and express any intelligible idea.

The long and short of it is that I am not, I have never been, a public animal. Tomorrow, I deluded myself, shielded by my beard, I would once more revert to the person I had always longed to remain: a pedestrian lost in the clouds, fascinated by the tiniest creatures and basically indifferent to the largest.

I was now only waiting for an opportunity; it was, alas, the most distressing: Emmanuel Liev's death, which occurred a few weeks before his eighty-ninth birthday, in the serenity of his rural home.

He had not been the 'inventor' of the Network of Sages, since the credit for that belonged to Vallauris; but, except on that point, he was everything for us. It was his wisdom which had obtained a hearing for the Network, and gained for it each of its successes; from then on, we had had to deal with a world-wide organization, to which the presence alone of the 'Old Man' gave strength and cohesion; his death clearly demanded the revision of structures and functions. For want of a personality of the same stature, it would be necessary to set up an international committee with members of sufficient quality and repute to fill the void left by Emmanuel; a more fully-staffed secretariat was also required, with central headquarters, regional offices, local committees, a budget.

All this updating – necessary as it probably was, I'm prepared to admit – took place amid innumerable negotiations, consultations and a deal of razzmatazz. I know that this is the way things are done in all human assemblies, in the holiest of congregations, in the most sacrosanct of caucuses . . . But I found all that hard to put up with. I was far away, body and soul. Besides, since Emmanuel's death, I had let my beard grow. And no one, not even Clarence, not even Beatrice, saw in this anything else than a quaint old-fashioned form of mourning.

S

I spent the summer of mists and storms, which preceded Beatrice's fifteenth birthday and my return to the laboratory, at Les Aravis in the Alps of Upper Savoy, where for four generations my family has owned a piece of land on a mountain side, a cow barn, a cave and a shepherd's hut, all neglected and with no road to get there. Already in my parents' day, we chose to spend our holidays in more congenial resorts, and the property remained deserted; in my entire childhood I only spent one short afternoon there; we were in the neighbourhood and my father wanted to make sure the site was 'still there' and the barn still standing; that was all, and I didn't think I'd retained the slightest memory of it.

So what sudden impulse made me think of this scrap of cold earth as a lost homeland? What voice had whispered to me one night that it was there, of all places, that I would let my beard grow, that it was there, at Les Aravis, between a barn and a rocky mountain side, that I would take refuge, in search of peace when the time came?

Neither Clarence nor Beatrice accompanied me, each preferring to go her own way and enjoy the *dolce far niente* of the seaside rather than endure the discomforts of my mountain retreat. It is true I had to sleep on a makeshift bed while the workmen I'd hurriedly engaged converted the barn into some semblance of a house and made the mule track into a road up which I could just about drive a car; I only asked them to undertake the heavy work, as I was determined to have a go myself, over the years, in my amateurish fashion, at the internal fixtures and fittings.

Frankly, I was finding my smooth hands and clean-shaven face smacked too much of the townee for my liking. Some people, even those closest to me, must have thought I was going through one of those crises on which modern confessors have bestowed a string of Greek names; if you're to take their word for it, every stage of one's life, every love affair, is a symptom requiring a remedy, something to be spoken of in concerned whispers. Clarence used to say, when we first got to know each other, that I was fundamentally old-fashioned, an anachronism. She was not far wrong, I hanker after those times, which I have only known at second hand, through books, when a man could still speak of vague yearnings or of feeling stifled, without anyone accusing him of having bats in the belfrey.

Of course, I missed my wife and daughter that summer; but I had a greater need of grassy paths, the animal smell of the earth, solitude, and the peace of the mountain-tops; I gazed at Mont Blanc facing the sunrise, when the whole landscape is one motionless pastel; I gazed at it again by night, preferably a moonless night, when the snow only owes its whiteness to its eternity.

When night really falls at Les Aravis, the only sounds are those of insects in search of their loves, and I took pleasure in distinguishing them, just as other people like to name the stars.

I slept little, and without desire.

*

At Les Aravis that summer, my sole daily link with the distant agitation of the world was an unwieldy, crackling, antiquated radio, that I switched on first thing in the morning, while I sat over my breakfast of cream cheese topped with honey and sprinkled with blueberries, waiting for the workmen to arrive.

It was seated thus that I heard, at the end of July, about the tragic events in Naïputo. Tragedies are to history what words are to thought, you never know if they are its cause, or simply its reflection. Because I had once happened to be a shocked eye-witness, I knew that a thousand minor expressions of anger had occurred, each, in its own way, heralding the tragedy; but there is, alas, a pollution threshold beyond which noises are not heard, and a point when the dead are not counted. If I speak bitterly of this, it is because I am convinced that for a long time the disease could have been cured; but all that time, it was neglected.

Here I am again, giving way to the senile, irritating temptation to preach to my contemporaries, when I had made it my duty to stick to facts . . .

So, to get back to them: during the evening of 27 July, a riot broke out in the Motodi district, inhabited by the tribe of that name; there were the usual accusations, by now routine and ritual: 'sterilization', 'castration', 'discrimination', 'genocide' – I retain the quotation marks simply to emphasize my reservations about these crude formulations, but these are merely the reservations of a sheltered observer; in Naïputo every word boomed out like the thump of a battering-ram.

What I had been able to see of the villagers' anger on the banks of the Nataval was still half-hearted, fairly harmless, its target simply the pock-marked façade of a rural health centre. How could my brief, pathetic experience enlighten me on what was happening in Naïputo? Can a bee-sting on a probing finger give any real idea of the fury of a violated hive?

The riot was said to have broken out simultaneously in thousands of alleyways with the rioters then converging on the centre of the capital, ransacking everything, setting fire to villas, shopping malls, banks, embassies.

Near the presidential palace, terrified soldiers fired into the crowd, the rioters fell in their hundreds, but others poured out of the side roads, leapt over the wall, managing to break down the little gate known as 'the gardeners' entrance'. The angry Motodis swarmed in. Armed with sticks, knives, a few revolvers or rifles, they soon occupied the palace and every one of its rooms; the head of state, who was giving a reception, was massacred with all his family, his friends and most of his guests. Before dawn, the official Radio-Television, the newly-inaugurated International Communications Centre, as well as most of the public buildings, had been looted and set on fire.

As soon as this news spread, the army disintegrated, every commissioned and non-commissioned officer, every soldier hurried back to his tribal region, the only place where he could feel safe. Naïputo was a grid of unapproachable ghettos, where the massacres continued without respite, extending by degrees to all the provinces.

What roused the rest of the world were the thousands of tourists of all nationalities scattered throughout the country; several hundreds were said to have gathered in a large central hotel. How could help be got to them? The country's authorities were by now practically non-existent, the forces of law and order had broken up into rival gangs, or, according to the cruel expression of one commentator, 'returned to their original elements'. The airports were closed, communications with the rest of the world had completely collapsed, and in all probability most of the embassies had been stormed.

Chanceries maintained a funereal silence. Capitals conferred as to what attitude to adopt.

To intervene? But at which points in this immense conflagration? And by what means? And against whom?

To send out warnings? But which responsible individuals were still at their posts, or still alive to take note of them?

To wait and observe? But every wasted hour could mean the death of hundreds of foreigners . . .

Naturally, every country was thinking in the first place of its own nationals. This is not a criticism, I am simply stating that in the North, as in the South, one worries first about the fate of one's own, that's a fact, I am blaming no one. Moreover, what did I myself do before anything else, as soon as I heard the news? I rushed to phone Clarence, who was with her parents in Sète, to assure myself that my journalist-partner was not entertaining any idea of going to observe this carnage at close range!

T

Of all the bloody upheavals that affected the countries of the South in the course of the preceding decades, what was it that caused the tragic events in Naïputo to be the watershed, the turning-point, the 'Sarajevo of the new century', as a present-day historian has described it?

The sudden and unexpected collapse of all authority, the unleashing of violence, the open hostility towards the North, and everything that represents or symbolizes it, all this was understandably disarming and bewildering, as much for the general public as for those in authority. But more serious still was the fact that all the ingredients for the tragedy existed, without exception, with the same potential for horror, for unpredictable madness, in ten, twenty, a hundred other Naïputos throughout the world!

Everywhere the said 'sterilization' had wrought its havoc, everywhere the necessary conditions for huge uprisings could be observed, everywhere the same resentment against the North and its local 'henchmen' was growing visibly. With accusations that an impartial observer would not have found convincing – but you don't convince a mob, you inflame it; there was legitimate fury and some appearance of evidence; that was sufficient. That sufficed.

It would be unjust not to add that individuals such as Foulbot and his emulators only exacerbated a situation that was already, and had long been, irremediably compromised; they did not invent poverty or corruption, the arbitrary or the many forms of segregation; they did not dig the North–South Divide – the 'horizontal fault-line – with their own hands; in their own minds, these sorcerer's apprentices were perhaps seeking for cures for these evils; but their invention was the fuse needed to set the powder-keg alight.

In quoting the comparison with Sarajevo, I am aware that I have adopted a common, fallacious habit of thinking. The person who sets out to tell the history of a war, finds himself constrained to put a date to the outbreak of hostilities, and to point to some irreparable act. But my sphere is that of my scientific studies rather than of History, so that for me such comparisons are of little help to understanding. I tend to think that serious upheavals lead a long existence underground. This is the way it is with cataclysms, as with insidious evils. They are not born, they break out. Just as wars do.

Yes, why deny it, I am thinking once again of the larvae of insects. This is a world with which I am familiar, which provides me with my sole terms of reference, my rare certainties: today's monsters were born the day before yesterday, but how many people can see the image beneath the mask? Nothing, in the grisly reality of the century of my old age, was unthinkable, unpredictable, unavoidable, fifty or ninety years ago; yet nothing was thought, nothing predicted, nothing avoided.

But what is the good of going back through the chain of causalities? What is the good of running counter to apparent logic? It is better to set down the turn of events methodically.

After three days of uncertainty came the confirmation of the most horrendous rumours: yes the slaughter continued, shootings and stabbings, not only in Naïputo but throughout the country; yes, hundreds of foreigners were dead, diplomats, tourists, expatriates, those travelling on business; and no, there was no indication that order would soon be restored. 'Those guilty of the atrocities will be punished,' it was declared in Washington, London, Berlin, Moscow, Paris and elsewhere; but it would first be necessary to put a face and a name to the guilty.

People came to regret the time when the North was divided and when, in order to attack one of the great powers, you had recourse to the sponsorship of the other, its weapons and its jargon.

For, more than the detail of the massacres, even more than the pictures and the evidence which gradually seeped out, what conferred on the tragic events in Naïputo their monstrous character, what was to linger long in our memories, was the impression the whole world gave of being helpless and disorientated, as if History had suddenly begun to gabble an incomprehensible language, a language re-suscitated from another era, or landed from another planet.

Today I can explain the phenomenon a little better. When a whole population thinks its survival threatened, you sometimes see the collapse of all the social codes which normally govern its behaviour. So, with so many communities, so many tribes feeling they were doomed to extinction, what barrages could possibly contain their fury?

Naïputo was but one stage on a long *via dolorosa*. Scarcely had a semblance of order been restored, with each ethnic group confined within its own territory, than other tragedies erupted in other regions, following the same bloody pattern. Historians speak nowadays of the 'Naïputo syndrome'; at the time people talked of 'an epidemic'. The latter word is incorrect. When the eggs of the same scorpion hatch out one after the other, you can't call it an epidemic, in the strict sense of the word. But there was doubtless a copy-cat phenomenon which Gulliver would certainly have remarked on, had he lived in our times; when one sees, on a billion screens, a Big-Ender slaughtering a Little-Ender, all the Little-Enders in the world feel threatened and many a Big-Ender discovers his own aptitude for murder.

Are not specialists familiar with the mimicry of pyro-maniacs, which is amplified by the media? Those pictures of mobs calling for the death of the 'sterilizers' could not remain without an echo among peoples suffering from the same evil.

After Naïputo, whose turn would be next? Whether clear-thinking or grief-stricken, people were sniffing out 'symptoms', 'tell-tale signs', 'requisite conditions', 'portents', nearly anywhere. If you were to believe them, few countries would be spared.

For a time these tragic events kept me apart from Clarence. We had the same concept of the dangers, but these inspired her with new reasons for continuing the battle, while I was more anxious than ever to get back to my life in the laboratory. As long as talking had any meaning, I had contributed a few words. As long as wisdom still had a part for me to play, I had stepped on to the stage. But now we were living in the age of madness, I was nothing but an intruder, out-of-date, a relic of the past, an anachronism – what was the use of deluding oneself? Why appear to be opposing the wave of hatred when the impotence of the most powerful was plain for all to see?

I reasoned in accordance with my temperament, and Clarence in accordance with hers. I admired her, she did not blame me for anything, we discussed things without acrimony. But our paths diverged.

She had got it into her head to set up in the most turbulent regions 'Committees of Sages', to be affiliated to the Network, and which, by influencing public opinion and governments, by the respect which they inspired in everyone, would form so many 'barrages' to contain the rising violence. This task of global proportions caused Clarence to be ceaselessly travelling from continent to continent. Paris was, at the best, simply a frequent stopover.

For my part, during the same period, I had had to undertake a quite different sort of move, which must seem laughable to today's reader, but which demanded of me a constant effort of adaptation.

When I had confirmed with the Director of the Museum my decision to return 'home', he had repeated that I was always welcome there; but added, without appearing to set any conditions, that it would suit him, as well as my colleagues, if I could accept a slight redeployment: rather than continuing in charge of coleoptera, as I had been till then, perhaps I would agree to direct, for a year or two, a research group on lepidoptera.

'Butterflies?' my first reaction was one of surprise and some disdain. I am not more insensitive than the next man to these creatures' prettiness, or the elegance of their flight; they can even achieve genuine magnificence in certain lights. Only I had always preferred to study the types of beauty that are not so obvious to the naked eye.

'Yes, butterflies,' the Director repeated, and in his mouth as in mine this common appellation sounded slangy, accompanied by the obligatory scornful clearing of the throat. 'I'm suggesting this as there's a vacancy, but I won't insist, I know that younger people than you and me would hesitate to make such a departure from their favourite subjects.' He did not insist, but without insisting he threw out a discreet challenge, for me to launch out into a new field of research at such an advanced age. 'I am well aware,' he went on, 'that at thirty you were already an authority on coleoptera, and you still are, in spite of the years you have taken off. You only have to say the word and I'll give you back this sector.' The person who had been in charge during my absence, would willingly step aside, he added, most unconvincingly.

I understood. 'Butterflies, it shall be!' I did not want my return to upset newly acquired positions. And then I was stimulated by the challenge. I felt myself perfectly capable of exploring new paths, and I was anxious to prove this.

Don't let's exaggerate, you will say, I was not changing my profession, not even my subject. I was still among the insects. But between a scarab and an astyanax, there is about as much similarity as between an eagle and a chimpanzee. During my entomological studies, I had, it is true, studied all the orders and sub-orders, the lepidoptera as well as the diptera, megaloptera or apocrita. But it had simply been a general survey, and it had been many decades ago. And then, as I have already had occasion to point out, with my three hundred and sixty thousand species of coleoptera, I already had enough to occupy my time! However, that need be no obstacle, I told myself, I will give myself a refresher course, even if I have to plunge once more into all the old classics since Linnaeus.

So it happened that in the course of my reading I came

across the Urania moths. They had probably been mentioned in my presence in a lecture, the name was not unfamiliar to me. But I knew nothing of their robe or their habits.

As big as a child's hand, with metallic green, brilliant black, and sometimes also reddish-orange stripes, and with a white border at the back, the Urania can be found in different parts of the globe, from the Pacific to Madagascar, from India to the Amazon. The species which particularly caught my attention is the one known as *Urania riphius*, and which is found in Central America.

Scientists who have taken an interest in the Urania have managed to observe an astonishing, spectacular phenomenon: on certain days of the year, these moths gather in tens of thousands of places where the forest meets the ocean, then they fly straight ahead for hundreds of nautical miles, until, finding no island on which to land, they fall exhausted into the sea and drown.

Certain females lay their eggs in the forest before the migration, thereby ensuring the survival of the species; but most of them fly off still swollen with eggs, so including their offspring in their collective suicide.

The flight of the Urania fascinated me from the moment I set eyes on the report of the first observations. I wondered if this journey into oblivion reflected a 'breakdown' in the instinct for survival, a genetic derangement, a tragic 'error in transmission' of the coded signs that seem to govern these migrations; one could multiply the hypotheses.

Blessed moment in the life of a researcher when he discovers a new passion. At this stage of my career, I had need of one. I was already so obsessed by my subject that I easily succeeded in convincing the dozen or so students whose work I was supervising, to devote a portion of their time to Urania. With no intention of deceiving them, I held out hopes of a possible trip to Costa Rica. But I didn't manage to obtain the necessary funds for a real study mission. If I had overcome this difficulty, I wonder how I could have left Paris – that is Beatrice – for the months that such a research project would have entailed, at a time when Clarence was so often away.

I often still regret not having made this trip. But, at my age, I take comfort in the thought that observation *in situ* would have been instructive, but tedious, and that it would doubtless have added nothing to the facts already known; it was perfectly conceivable and legitimate for my team to study the observations made by others in order to assimilate them and attempt an interpretation.

We were able to formulate certain hypotheses. They formed the subject of a monograph which the circumstances did not allow me time to publish and which is still to be found in one of my drawers. In it, I expressed the opinion that the behaviour of the Urania is not the result of a loss of the instinct for self-preservation, but, on the contrary, of the survival of an ancestral reflex which leads these creatures to a place where they used to reproduce in former times, perhaps an island which has since disappeared; thus, their apparent suicide could be an involuntary act, caused by the failure of the instinct for survival to adapt to new circumstances; these ideas intrigued my students, but certain colleagues proved sceptical as to their formulation.

The Urania occupied the best part of the first two years of

my return to my scientific career. The rest of the time I devoted to Les Aravis, where Beatrice sometimes accompanied me and helped with the work. The house was taking shape and acquiring a soul, although with rather rudimentary comfort; as a sole concession to modern gadgetry, I had installed a useful device which allows me to switch on the heating by remote control, so avoiding the problem of going into a vast icy area. Two weeks never went by without my going there; even snow-bound roads could not deter me.

Clarence had not yet been, but we had planned for the three of us to spend a month there together in the summer; a peaceful, sedentary, stay-at-home, recuperative month. These words aroused in my companion a yearning which she forced herself to silence. Sometimes, in the darkness of our bedroom, she confessed to a certain weariness, but she had chosen to be a cog in the machine, she no longer felt the right to stop, even for a short break. On no account would she want any weakness of hers to interfere with her struggle.

Nevertheless, I had managed to extract from her the promise of this month of peace, using in particular the argument that our daughter would not agree much longer to spend the holidays with 'her old folks', and that it was her mother's duty to see more of her regularly, talking and listening to her. In spite of my respect for Clarence's dedication, as well as the way she managed her time, I was determined to exert all necessary pressure to force her to keep her promise.

Alas! I did not need to use my influence, nor my doubtful powers of persuasion. An unknown hand was to decide for us, with the most implacable efficacity.

Clarence had left on a trip to Africa. At the last moment, taking care not to warn me, she had suddenly decided to stop off for a couple of days in Naïputo. It is true that for several months no killings had been reported, but the situation remained unpredictable, unsettled, 'volatile'.

She wanted to resume contact with the country, shake up the local branch of the Network which was not managing to make itself heard, and take this opportunity of seeing people she had met on previous trips, in particular Nancy Uhuru, the owner of the 'Mansion', with whom she had made friends when we stayed there ten years ago.

When she arrived at the airport, where a semblance of order reigned, but which was almost deserted except for the throngs of beggars, she was surprised to have to explain to a very young taxi driver how to get to Uhuru Mansion. Her suspicions ought already to have been roused. And all the more so when the man warned her hardly anyone travelled on that road any more.

However, the taxi was only two minutes away from its destination when it was intercepted by men in military uniform; the driver was forced to stop at a makeshift road-block – a huge branch, an empty barrel, a heap of stones, and, in particular, machine guns levelled at them. It was probably one of the marauding gangs of soldiers who were roaming the whole country. The foreign press said that they were no longer operating in the neighbourhood of the capital; evidently this was not the case.

Clarence was ordered out. Her driver happened to belong to the same ethnic group as the brigands, who let him keep his car, simply 'confiscating' his passenger's luggage. When she protested, shouting and threatening them, and then when she tried to snatch her handbag containing her passport, keys and papers from one of the assailants, she received a blow from a rifle-butt on the back of her head, which felled her to the ground, unconscious.

The driver dragged her back to the car and after interminable arguments obtained permission to proceed on his way.

Fortunately Nancy Uhuru was at the guest house, as expansive and cheerful as ever, despite the delapidated state of her 'Mansion', where, it goes without saying, no guest had ventured for ages. She took Clarence to a hospital run by the Red Cross, where a serious cranial injury was diagnosed.

When the accident occurred, Nancy was too preoccupied with the fate of the victim and the treatment she needed, to try to contact me; moreover, she hadn't kept my address or telephone number and no papers had been found on Clarence that could give any idea of my whereabouts.

So, for five days I had gone about my daily routine, without the slightest foreboding, without a shred of anxiety, all the more so since my companion was in the habit of leaving me for long periods without keeping in touch.

Eventually, I found a message on my answerphone, from the headquarters of the Red Cross in Geneva, simply leaving a telephone number and asking me to call them back urgently.

What was the worst moment of all? Not when I learnt of the attack on Clarence and the seriousness of her condition. No, I had been afraid of that, the minute I received the message, and my lips feverishly muttered, like an incantation, 'Only let her still be alive!' Neither was the worst moment when I saw her lying, still unconscious, trussed up like a mummy, surrounded by gleaming, humming instruments. No, the worst moment was when, having dialled the Geneva number, and listening to it ring four times, I heard someone pick up the phone and I had to give my name and wait for the verdict.

'I have bad news for you, but the person concerned is alive and her condition is stable. You are, I believe, Clarence's companion . . .'

Alive. She was alive. That was all I prayed for.

The voice informed me briefly of what had happened, and the treatment she had received so far. They thought to fly her back to Paris within seventy-two hours.

'If the delay had been longer, we would have suggested you go to her bedside.'

The man who was speaking to me was clearly accustomed to dealing with the families of people involved in accidents, his serious voice did not attempt to raise unreasonable hopes, and so proved reassuring. He anticipated the questions I could have asked, circumvented them, and finally succeeding in persuading me to wait patiently as long as possible, so that I wouldn't get in the way of the ambulance crews.

'I would suggest that you just meet us at the hospital.'

Three days later, I was sitting on a plastic chair, with my head in my hands, my elbows on my knees, at the bedside of my unconscious companion. Beside me, Beatrice sat staring silently, frowning hard, as if she were taking a course in solemnity.

During the first few days, I sat there uncomfortably, fidgeting, letting my mind wander, going over images from the past. Then I began to bring a book with me; from time to time, when I was alone with Clarence, I tried to talk aloud to her, reassuring her about her condition; I had read that patients, even when in a coma, could hear and understand what was being said around them, and even if they did not remember when they regained consciousness, it raised their morale. I mentioned this to the neurologist who was looking after her, he didn't really try to disillusion me. 'It's possible, if the coma is not too deep . . .' But the glint in his eyes seemed to imply, 'If it doesn't help the patient, it can help the relatives.'

It is true that, during those long days, Beatrice and I were much more vulnerable than Clarence. Then I remembered something my companion had said during one of our first meetings. I had just told her that when you love someone your greatest wish is to depart this life first. She had retorted, frivolously, 'Dying is a selfish action!' Was the state in which she had got into any less selfish? She could have passed from the unconcern of the coma to the unconcern of death, with no regard for the man who loved her and who, once she had gone, would never have the same taste for life again; deserting me like this seemed just a bit casual.

You can see that my feelings for Clarence at that time were not all affectionate. I was more angry with her for having exposed herself to this attack than I was with the stranger who had struck her. The latter, in my eyes, had neither existence nor responsibility, he was one of those frantic creatures, growing daily more numerous, and whose numbers would go on increasing, who were as much victims as persecuters, monsters born from the chaos and perpetuating it. But what excuse could Clarence have?

The look in my eyes would condemn, but the next moment I was gazing fondly at her again, promising never to leave her in future and to make allowances for all her weaknesses, if she would only do me the favour of surviving.

Her accident had occurred in mid-March, on the 14th to be exact; and it was not till the afternoon of 2 June that she moved her lips again. She did not say anything coherent yet, but this was the first sign of her return to life. It is true that, from the beginning, the doctors had reassured me as to the essential: she did not appear to be brain-damaged; we just had to wait, she would certainly move again, she would speak, she would get up. But for me, this was all so much eyewash; even more than the doctors' talk, I was waiting for what Clarence would say.

On that same 2 June – date for evermore blessed – she opened her eyes, and I could see that inside her bandages the intelligence which had captivated me was still present.

From then on, I could watch her being reborn, hour by hour; I talked to her at length, it did not seem to tire her to listen to me, occasionally smiling, showing approval, doubt, speaking little and slowly herself, but after a few days, distinctly enough for me to be amply reassured about her intellectual faculties.

*

She was to suffer for a long time the after-effects of this attack, all the future years were to be for both of us a patient process of rehabilitation, a slow recovery. But in this misfortune we could eventually see our luck: 'While others decline with age,' Clarence said, 'I find at fifty the privilege enjoyed by children, of progressing step by step, relearning actions and pleasures.'

She said this with so fresh, so radiant a face that she finally persuaded me that everyone needed a good fall before starting on the second stage of their lives. Individuals, human societies, and the species also. Perhaps this is the price we have to pay before we can get our second wind.

V

It was in July of the year Twenty of the Century of Beatrice, and Clarence, clinging to my arm, was taking her morning walk from one end of the living-room to the other, when a news-flash breathlessly announced the death of Abdane, 'that most devout general', who for the last thirty years, had been Rimal's despotic Head of State, Rimal being one of the richest countries in the South.

A few years earlier, the passing of such a person would merely have given rise to a legitimate sense of relief; in our youth we had experienced periods of euphoria when we had amused ourselves watching similar Molochs go down one after the other, like monstrous ninepins. But times had changed us, we had learned to fear chaos more than tyranny, we were sorry and ashamed, but too much had collapsed since Naïputo, too much savagery had resulted, too much regression, for change in itself to inspire us with any enthusiasm, for us to be lured by slogans. It would be laughable, would it not, to ask if it was I who was growing old, or History, but the answer still does not seem clear to me.

When Abdane rose to power he had put an end to a totally corrupt monarchy; he had said 'liberty', 'republic' and these thousand-fold violated virgins had regained their virginity; we needed to believe, Abdane had let us believe. When, shortly after he came to power, he had shot a too ambitious deputy, we had looked away, convinced that we mustn't condemn his whole experience on the strength of this one act of self-defence. Convinced also – but at the time we did not calculate the full implication of our attitude – that as children of the North, the privileged 'haves' and former colonizers, we had no right to lecture the people of the South.

I repeat, in no way could we see the implication of our attitude. We – that is I, my generation, and those around us – were appalled if a Ukrainian opponent was silenced, but if a Rimalian was thrown into a dungeon, we suddenly rediscovered forgotten notions of non-intervention. Anyone would think decolonization had begun with Pontius Pilate. So that was possibly how the North-South Divide, that 'horizontal fault-line', was created in people's minds, the line dividing moral values, or, as a forgotten philosopher from my childhood would have said, 'the dividing line between men and savages'. Even at the time when apartheid was receding, a similar notion of 'separate development' had gained ground on a global scale: on the one hand, civilized nations, with their citizens, their institutions; on the other, kinds of 'Bantustans', picturesque reserves governed according to their own customs, that you stood and gawked at.

I remember meeting a Rimalian academic who now missed the time when people still spoke of 'a civilizing mission'; at least then it was still admitted that everyone was civilizable, even if only in theory. More pernicious, according to him, was the 'attitude which consists of proclaiming that everyone is civilized, by definition, and to the same degree, that all values are equal, that every human being is a humanist, and that, consequently, everyone must follow the path prescribed by his roots'.

The young man hid his anger behind a veil of cool ironical ridicule: 'Formerly, we had to put up with contemptuous rascism; nowadays we suffer from respectful racism. Indifferent to our aspirations, gushing over our gaucheries, fascinated by our mutilations. The most loathsome customs, relics of the past, the most degrading mutilations become a "cultural heritage". To each his century!'

Such were the sentiments of many Rimalians, especially in the best educated circles. Abdane, on the contrary, congratulated himself that his specificity, his authenticity was being recognized; he went about draped in loose traditional robes, to indicate he intended to play the power game according to his own rules, of which his ancestors obligingly approved. And when their age-old voices were sometimes silent, Abdane knew how to act the ventriloquist, and gladly forged them.

For long he had had sufficient tricks up his sleeve. His subjects were docile; and we people of the North were under his spell. Corrupt? Depraved behind the high walls of his palaces? But in the streets he bludgeoned the populace into collective worship. He had installed his countless brothers and cousins in all the important posts? In the North, we would have talked of nepotism; in the South, it was called 'family solidarity'. Many notions needed to be translated in this way as soon as they crossed the North-South Divide. It was Clarence who pointed out to me that a European who opposed an autocratic regime was called a 'dissident'; but when one day she had spoken of 'an African dissident' in an article, an editor, deeming the term incorrect, had automatically replaced it by 'opponent', without even feeling the need to consult her, as if he were correcting a stylistic error or spelling mistake. In the same order of ideas, a worker from the South, settling in the North, was called 'an immigrant'; a worker from the North, settling in the South, was known as 'an expatriate'. Not to be confused!

I would not wish to multiply these examples, my sole intention here is to remind readers who are under thirty, or those who have forgotten, of the atmosphere that reigned then, of the smoke-screen that descended as soon as it was a question of the upheavals in the South.

The uprising against Abdane took place a little before dawn. Officers of the guard had entered the general's harem and slaughtered him and the wife who was spending that night with him; other soldiers had simultaneously seized the television building to announce the death of the 'infidel, apostate, hypocritical tyrant, lackey of the corrupt West, responsible for the sterilization'; and to call on the people to rebel. Their message was immediately heard; probably passed on by word of mouth through fellow conspirators positioned in various districts. The first attacks were on those nearest to the general, members of his clan, his collaborators; later in the day, and no one knew whether this was part of the rebels' plan, or whether this had got out of hand, the rioters started attacking modern buildings, where foreign companies had their offices. Then they swarmed into the residential districts of the city where expatriates' villas alternated with those of rich Rimalians; then there was an orgy of murder, rape, torture, destruction; much more destruction, moreover, than looting, as the surviving eye-witnesses remarked; the rioters demanded nothing, stole nothing, no greed detained them in their search for vengeance.

It is important to make this point clear, for people talked then of a 'new Naïputo' – and even today I come across this expression in certain inexact accounts. Is it not somewhat simplistic to describe in this way any sudden explosion that leads to chaos? There was, however, this difference between the two occurrences, which Emmanuel Liev had referred to in his New York speech, and which only those close to the Network and its concerns noticed at the time. Put simply, I would say that Naïputo still had women but no girls; in Rimal, the rebels, beginning with the army officers, felt condemned to spend their entire lives without wives, without children, without homes.

Why in Rimal exactly? Because it was in this rich and at the same time reactionary country that the 'substance' and its related methods were used very early and on a large scale. Nowhere was belief in the absolute superiority of the male so indisputable, and nowhere, in the countries of the South, was modern technology, principally in the field of medicine, so accessible. With no moral or financial safeguards, the methods of selective births had spread very early, very fast, in every stratum of the population, whether settled or nomadic. In Naïputo, in the worst year, there was still one girl out of every five live births; in Rimal, for several successive years, the ratio was less than one girl to twenty boys – that is naturally only an estimate, Abdane being one of the first leaders to forbid the publication or even the collection of population statistics.

Stupidity? Criminal negligence? These were the words used by the press in the first days following the fall of the master of Rimal; in this respect, however, he was no different from other rulers at that time. Very few were capable of seriously contemplating questions which would only be asked in fifteen or thirty years time; the majority preferred to leave them as a poisoned legacy to the ones who would have the arrogance to succeed them.

Moreover, everyone believed Rimal would remain immune from the violent upheavals in the South. People made a pretence of cursing Abdane's firm grip, but in view of what was happening all over the place, they blessed him silently.

Once – it was, as I remember, three or four years before the uprising – a human rights organization had reported eight hundred and fifty executions for rape in the course of the preceding twelve months; the tyrant had replied that this was the law of his country, the tradition of his people, and that he would not let himself be dragged along the paths leading to perdition. A speech which it was becoming more and more difficult to answer, especially since it was certain knowledge that rape was no longer a common individual crime but the expression of a universal aggressivity whose spread everyone feared.

Perhaps it can be better understood nowadays how confused Clarence and I were on that July morning. Already by the evening, and especially the next day, when the stories of the massacres became known, there was no longer much room for ambiguity: we had, alas! to agree with those around us, those in charge, the media, the man in the street, who, while expressing reserves about the fallen leader and his methods, were reduced to wishing for a return, as if it were a golden age, to the era of corruption, despotism, duplicity.

There was, by virtue of its horror, its very disproportion, something epic in the fury that overwhelmed Rimal. I would not want, with this word, to glorify the crime, nor aggrandize the destructive folly. No! I am simply trying to explain that, from the beginning, the events acquired an apocalyptic significance. As if something irreparable had just occurred, as if the whole of mankind had suddenly become aware of a nightmare which it had more or less succeeded in pretending did not exist. There were, to be sure, the pictures of the horror, the number of the dead, including thousands of foreigners – even those governments who prided themselves on their *'glasnost'* did not dare confirm the figures. But more than that, there was a feeling that a part of the world, the largest part, the most populated, was about to become a no-go area, a limbo where no one could henceforth venture, with which no exchange would soon be possible.

And, at one fell swoop, the North became aware that 'the planet down South' which it had been in the habit of considering a dead weight, was part of its own body, and it began to experience the deliquescence of the South like a mutilation, or worse, like gangrene.

W

It was rather cold comfort, but the crack in the world was to have the effect of improving matters in my own household.

Between Clarence and Beatrice, I had never been able to detect the slightest collusion – there was no antagonism either, I may add, nor any friction; to me, they seemed to remain irremediably strangers to each other. I made every effort to bring them closer; I used to take every opportunity of leaving them alone together, hoping this would give rise to whispered confidences . . . A waste of time, my family remained a triangle without a base, Clarence and I, Beatrice and I, forming the two verticals, and this, as I have already pointed out, began before my daughter's birth, when she was simply an idea, a wish, mine alone, rather than my partner's, who only bore her to satisfy me.

It was to me that Beatrice confessed, when she first fell madly in love. I was so touched, so flattered that it never occurred to me to behave like a father, if behaving like a father means making some suitable remarks, using my authority to preach to her – this paternal role, written by others, did not attract me; I had something better, the privilege of her confidence, two tears shed on my shirt, two tears that I covered with my hand, as if forbidding them to dry.

It was my path, too, which Beatrice followed, by choosing to study biology, rather than journalism.

Such was the state of affairs in my family, when Clarence's accident occurred, and upset the established order. As long as the mother was a mother and the daughter was a daughter, their relationship had been cool, somewhat starchy. The picture which I made every effort to conjure up, that of a beaming father and mother, arms around each other, leaning over a cradle, had never had any reality; I have another framed picture on my table as I write these lines: father and daughter, arms around each other, leaning over a wheel-chair. That is how we were united, by virtue of this reversal of roles; Beatrice was affectionately maternal, Clarence resolutely daughterly; friends at last.

After such a long gestation, their relationship could not reasonably stagnate in still waters. It was immediately ardent, insatiable, like the love of a faithful sailor, home from the sea. And fruitful.

One day, on returning from the Museum, I saw them in an unusual position: Clarence in her chair, dictating a rush of sentences to Beatrice, a scribe squatting on the floor, in front of the screen, conscientiously tapping out her mother's outpourings. A sight which was to become familiar. Sometimes, when my partner fell silent, our daughter ventured a question or an objection. They argued, grew heated, revised, corrected together. A corporate work took shape. Their 'child', of which I was, at best, the godfather.

Any other person than myself would have felt threatened, dethroned; I am not like that, their reunion delighted me. I watched them; I listened to them; if I wanted to interrupt them, or call them, I would say, 'Girls!' delighted to group them together, without distinction of age, under this same protective word.

When their series of articles was published, in a quality daily, their topicality assured them a vast, attentive readership. Their original idea was not new: there is, with human societies, as with individuals, a male principle, which is the principle of aggression, and a female principle, which is the principle of perpetuation. Certain men suffer from an excess of male hormones, or from the presence of a supernumerary male chromosome; these beings are sometimes intelligent, but their intelligence is said to be distorted by extreme aggressiveness, and often put to criminal use; court records would show countless similar cases. Are we not in the presence of such a phenomenon, asked Clarence and Beatrice, but on a global scale? Because of some un-scrupulous scientists, because too of this North-South Divide, which no one was able to warn against, might we not have provoked for communities, ethnic groups, peoples, and possibly the entire human species, a gigantic derangement?

I do not want to discuss the value of this thesis; its importance lies less in its scientific rigour than in the way it emphatically fitted the state of current events, in the face of which our finest minds were defenceless. So, might not the peoples of the South have been transformed, under our very eyes, into mutants drunk with violence, since deprived of all normal existence and with no future? To confirm such a concept, there was much more than mere appearances. Everyone had seen the distorted diagrams representing population by age groups, the scientific transcription of daily atrocities; from Naïputo to Rimal, the countless episodes of fire and sword were already landmarks in our memories; and everyone guessed that the near future would be more of the same.

When you suddenly find yourself on the other face of the mountain of horror, everything seems logical, obvious, expected, inescapable; yes, everything could most certainly have been foreseen, from the moment the North-South Divide was created, from the moment the secrets of life fell into the hands of the sorcerer's apprentices; already, in the last century, there were all the pre-indications of chaos; the cities which crumbled, one after the other, the nations which disintegrated, the absurd retreat towards past millennia, the expulsions, the encapsulations.

Cause and effect – what a brilliant subterfuge! you will say. Among the infinite number of possible turnings, who could have recognized in time the one leading to the apocalypse? My answer will be that I have known men and women who could read the secrets of the universe like an open book; some of them are no longer with us, some are still around, I still warm myself at the fire of their inspiration. Men and women who, as I have already said, could read in the larva the shape of the 'imago', the final, perfect insect.

But it is on the *imago* that I must fix my gaze for the space of a few paragraphs. Everyone today can see as well as me what the world has begun to look like, nothing of what I could describe is unfamiliar, nothing will surprise; but such is the absurd task that I have set myself – as a witness, forensic artist, recorder of epilogues.

Those who, like me, have known the age when there were no well-defined borders, when the whole world was linked by a thousand well-lit paths, how could they not be totally confused in this compartmentalized world! Never could I have believed that the expansion would be short-lived, that so many walls would arise, insurmountable walls, along the roads and in people's minds.

One after the other, the countries of the South shut themselves off, like lights being extinguished in an encampment at night. But it was not for a period of sleep, the dark set in for good, eyelids could no longer expect any dawn.

The last century had provided us with a hundred examples of societies which suddenly went mad. You took care to feel sympathy, but you got used to it, the world still spun screaming around in its course; too bad about those left behind, those sucked down in the quicksands, those out of breath from running. History was in a hurry, it could not stop to share in the bitter suffering . . . But where was History going then? With what was its rendezvous? And on what date?

So who could have dared predict the retrogression? Retrogression, a depressing idea, laughable, heretical, incongruous. People insist on regarding History as a river flowing peaceably through flat countryside, racing wildly in hilly terrain, and here and there tumbling over a waterfall. And what if its bed is not hollowed out in advance? And what if it is unable to reach the sea and it loses itself in the desert, in a maze of stagnant marshes?

Cynical words? I only hope that my Beatrice will be able to grow old in a regenerated world; and that, in the future, these cursed decades will be seen as enclosed in gigantic parentheses.

Even before the troubles in Rimal, certain countries in the

North advised their nationals against travelling to countries at risk. A discreet term, limited in principle to regions such as Naïputo which had already experienced their moment of murderous orgy.

Rimal, naturally, had never featured on their lists – had not General Abdane abolished insecurity, eradicated violence? No one would have insulted him by speaking of risks in connection with him. His brutal downfall, and the fate meeted out to foreigners who lived under his protection, meant that no destination was safe any more, once you'd crossed the latitude into hell.

Without any further attempt to spare diplomatic suscept-ibilities, there was a move to evacuate tens of thousands of families who had settled in the South. A few embassies still clung on to an ultimate distinction between countries in which violence had broken out and those where it was only 'latent'. These subtleties disappeared, however, in the stampede to save one's skin that infected the whole world.

A quite understandable reaction, but one which pre-cipitated the débâcle. At the sight of these thousands of expatriates hurriedly collecting their goods and crowding into the airports, how could the local people continue going about their daily business? Several countries, which up till then had been more or less peaceful, became frantic; after the exodus of the foreigners came that of the local élite, and even of ordinary people terrified of the future.

Even today, when we know much more about the origin of the troubles which have afflicted the planet, how many people still refuse to consider the peoples of the South as victims, and only retain two images of them: those migrant multitudes, very close at hand, too close to us; and, in the distance, those crazed hordes, determined to destroy a world which they no longer understood, and who, first and foremost, were punishing themselves. One day, perhaps, a tribunal of History will pronounce belated sentences for 'deprivation of a future'.

Here, in the North, we only feel the backlash of the troubles; let us spare an occasional thought for those who experience the direct impact. Let us think of those countries where no one dares venture any more, shut off from the outside world, fragmented into tribes set desperately at each other's throats in their common distress, abandoned by the best of their sons, surviving like weeds among the ruins. And, on the horizon, more ruins.

In Rimal, as in a full two-thirds of the planet, time now stands still. Planes no longer land, no longer take off, except for the occasional ancient bomber; the roads leading into infinity, which General Abdane had laid out at great expense, as if to keep the desert at bay, have disappeared in a few months, submerged beneath the avenging sands; the mines have reverted to caves, machines stand patiently dissolving in rust and oblivion; in the modern districts, buildings still stand, but blackened, scarred, most of them gutted, cynical monuments to a civilization that lasted for a day. Another millennium finished, say the stones, just one more.

From Rimal, from Naïputo, from the Near and Far East, from Africa, and also from the slums of the New World, men are still fleeing, whenever they can, by boat or on muleback. They are the last bearers of the ancient Enlightenment, they escape like the last words of a dying man.

To reach the North, north of the Mediterranean, north of the Rio Grande, no need of a compass, their elders have gone before, the road is inscribed in their genes, its hardships are sweet, its rigours forgiven in advance. In the countries which receive them, many talk of an invasion; but what's to be done, you don't cast a shipwrecked man back into the sea.

I remember once coming across a curious metaphor, from a well-intentioned pen. Our planet, said the author, is like a two-tier rocket. One part is uncoupled, falls to earth and disintegrates; the second is detached and having shed its load soars into space, intact.

Even when that text was published, it would have been easy to retort ironically, 'Just imagine what would happen if the lower planet disintegrated while remaining hooked to the upper one by a bolt that had not been properly unscrewed . . .?' But such were the naïve, shameful, petty illusions of my contemporaries; and yet they were legitimate, as are all instinctive reactions for survival.

X

I could not but be aware that the time for father and daughter to part hovered perpetually in the air. I only hoped I would not have to endure it in the old manner, giving Beatrice my arm at the door of a building, walking with her clumsily a few yards, then making way for another, returning to the ranks, having to put up with the glances people thought appropriate . . . No, I told myself, this is not the way to arrange such partings these days. There should be neither priest's chasuble nor mayoral scarf of office. No bride hanging on paternal arm, no guests. When the thing happened, it was not to be pinned down by a date.

As a final precaution, I had very early spoken my mind to my daughter, even before her first love affair: her room was her room, I had insisted, this house was her home, she could leave when she liked and return when it suited her, alone or with friends; however far she travelled, she would need to have, 'at the back of her mind', the comfort of a home port where she could keep at least a few of her childhood things. She was touched; had said 'yes' enthusiastically, and called me by all my favourite pet names. I was reassured and proud.

All things considered, life had not attacked everything I had built up. It had simply given the frail structure a little jolt. Just sufficient for it to remain a life.

*

When Beatrice began to go around with Morsi, I quickly took a liking to him. His father was Egyptian and his mother a native of Savoy; yet it was the latter who had insisted on giving him the unusual first name, that he himself loved to joke about. 'When I introduce myself, I say very quickly "I'm Morsi"; men think I say Marcel and women Maurice!' At our first meeting, I naturally told him about my one and only visit to his country, for the conference on the scarab beetle. He admitted that he had always lived in France or Switzerland, that he had only been to Cairo twice, for short holidays; and Clarence was disappointed to learn that he had never set foot in Alexandria, the city which she prided herself on hailing from.

'I thought your family came from Salonika,' Beatrice said in surprise.

'And I thought it was Odessa,' I added quite insincerely.

Clarence placed her hand on Morsi's shoulder.

'Explain to them that my native land is a galaxy of cities! Explain to them that you and I are born from the light of the East, and that the West did not awaken till our light shone on it! Tell them that our East has not always been plunged in darkness! Tell them about Alexandria and Smyrna and Antioch and Salonika and the Valley of the Kings and the Jordan and the Euphrates. But perhaps you cannot do this!'

She spoke with a mixture of exaggeration and derision and Morsi was sad, with the sadness one feels at the sight of a clown's tears.

However, he was not often sad. Beatrice had met him at the laboratory where she had just been taken on; he was considered the cleverest of the research team, but also the zaniest, an absurd combination which attracted her from the start. They had the same bronze complexion, were the same height, and within a few months of the same age; they gave the impression of having always lived hand in hand. With his short curly hair, his oval head copied from some Pharaonic bas-relief, and his frank but respectful laugh, Morsi soon became a part of our family scene.

His parents lived in Geneva, both specializing in pharmacology; he himself was our neighbour in Paris, having found a tiny studio flat near the Arènes de Lutèce. More than once I was about to suggest to him, through the intermediary of Beatrice, that he move in with us, but I never did so, I didn't feel I had the right to precipitate matters, nor to formalize them.

Out of an Eastern sense of decency, I suppose, Morsi never spent the night in our flat; Beatrice, on the other hand, was frequently absent, especially at weekends. And one day, on coming home from the Museum, I found her things in boxes near the door. Guessing my emotion, Clarence explained that our daughter, at twenty-five, needed to live full-time with a man. I was about to argue. I murmured a pitiful 'Why?' which hung in the air. Then I retired with dignity to my study, determined not to emerge until the boxes had been removed.

I who feared lest Beatrice's departure would be rooted in my memory by some ceremony . . . There was nothing but these boxes, piles of books, folded clothing, framed photographs, and then this room too carefully tidied, from now on kept in order by her absence. To distract myself, I went through my collection of coleoptera, sticking back some names that had become detached.

Only when I had tired myself out by dinner time, did I shed the two statutory tears, I was back to normal; that's life, when you commit yourself to love, you make no provision for the parting.

The next day, Beatrice and Morsi came for breakfast, a tactful touch which I appreciated. My daughter seemed light-hearted, more playful than usual, as if to tell me she still knew how to be a child, my child.

None of the four of us suspected she was already pregnant. I was to learn this some weeks later, in a roundabout fashion. The results of an investigation into the fate of the women of Rimalia and other countries in the South had just been published. It might have been supposed that, because of their increasing rarity, women would have been honoured, idolized, courted; they were simply more coveted. This is perhaps the worst image that future centuries will retain of us: these cloistered besieged women, the precious property of their tribes, prizes fought over in bloody quarrels; they could not walk in the street without escort for fear of rape and kidnap. 'We've gone back to the time of the Rape of the Sabine Women!' I commented.

Beatrice placed her hand on Morsi's, saying, 'I hope it will be a boy!' Coming from her, such a wish was so incongruous! However, that was not what struck me, but rather, how shall I put it, the blunt announcement of the news: I immediately rose to my feet, walked round the chair where my daughter was sitting, then leaned over her, placing my lips on her forehead and my hand on her still flat belly. 'I'm in my third month,' she laughed to give herself a countenance.

I watched Clarence out of the corner of my eye, she was as surprised as me, but she reacted differently.

'Is this really a good century to be born in?'

That evening, in our bedroom, I bitterly reproached her for these words. Whatever the dramatic, tragic events of our times, those are not the words to pronounce in front of a mother-to-be. Beatrice was on the threshold of an exciting, trying adventure; we should not be surrounding her with our anxieties; and was this the way to welcome the child who was to be born? Only one being in the world would be as dear to me as Beatrice: Beatrice's child. Even if I were tired of life, I would renew my lease for another twenty years just to see this little creature grow up, to take it for walks in the park, to see its little face light up at the sight of candy-floss.

Clarence snuggled up to me.

'You are all fire tonight,' she said. 'Hold me tight, I want to store up your love in myself, all your love, for me, for Beatrice, and for Beatrice's child.'

Love, as a form of escape, an embrace as an ultimate argument, pleasure by way of suspension of any further talk, could I complain of this way of changing the subject? Clarence was always able to win my body over to her cause; my thoughts would calm down until morning.

In the morning, moreover, she admitted I was right. If not substantially – she never shared my breathless wonderment at childhood – at least in the attitude to adopt in the presence of our daughter. Nevertheless she persisted in adding thoughtfully, by way of a footnote, '. . . But Beatrice is right to want a boy under the circumstances.'

'What circumstances? We aren't in Rimal, or in Naïputo, to the best of my knowledge!'

'No doubt, but we're all in the same boat. What evils will now be contained within boundaries? Hatred is contagious, and so can retrogression be.'

I have never been heedless of Clarence's views. She tended

to give pride of place to the most apocalyptic of all scenarios; History, alas! occasionally had the same annoying tendency. Neither of them strayed off into analyses; they simply pronounced verdicts.

Clarence and History, two characters in my life, often in collusion; but the one out of extreme lucidity, the other from extreme blindness.

Y

In accordance with her wish, Beatrice had a son, whom she named Florian. When, an hour after the birth, I went to visit her, I was astonished to observe armed policemen in the corridor. I had already seen, in the cinema rather than in real life, policemen in a hospital, keeping an eye on a sick prisoner, or guarding the victim of an attack, someone under threat. But in a maternity home? My first supposition was that a prisoner had just given birth. It was Morsi who enlightened me.

'It's on account of the rumours.'

'What rumours?'

Oh yes! Then I remembered. Rumours had been circulating for the past few months that baby girls were being kidnapped by gangs of sordid traffickers, to be 'sold' in countries where there was a shortage. I had shrugged my shoulders and, in a sense, I was not wrong. The paranoia created by these rumours was out of all proportion to the established facts. There has always been, over the years, a certain number of children and young women disappearing; no one has ever been able to prove, to the best of my knowledge, that the scale of such kidnappings had differed significantly during the years of which I am speaking.

Where I was wrong, on the other hand, was to have underestimated the extent of the fear which was spreading.

Perhaps I would have been more sensitive if Beatrice had had a daughter.

With hindsight, this fear was only too easy to understand. In the North, the generations without women were reaching maturity. I have already explained how the worst could have been avoided, and I repeat here that the imbalance between boys and girls was still moderate when compared with that in the South. All the same, it was not insignificant, and this, according to the specialists, was the cause of the sudden rise in delinquency among adolescents. Immediately following wars, certain societies had known periods when there were more women than men; in spite of the distress, in spite of the privations and imposition of quotas, it was, in the eyes of History, a question of periods of peace during which the human race got its second wind; up till now, societies in which young males were in overwhelmingly superior numbers had never been observed 'life size'.

If this imbalance had occurred in a normal environment, perhaps it could have been faced more calmly. This was decidedly not the case. After the events in Rimal, a wind of anxiety had blown through the world, century-old lines of exchange had been brutally snapped, in others the current flowed more slowly, the planet had clearly shrunk, shrivelled, like a diseased or over-ripe apple. Rimal had formerly been the standard-bearer of a certain prosperity; its downfall created a sensation, heralding as it did the coming of a new age, the age of retrogression.

I prefer this term to that of 'great depression', to which some of my unimaginative contemporaries remain attached. Not that I deny all similarity to the Black Friday of 1929, and all the old disquiets of the last century. But comparisons hide as much as they reveal, the century of Beatrice is similar to no other, even if, here and there, some of its horrifying characteristics, seem like those of the past.

Economists can explain better than I the way the collapse of the South upset the wealth of the North; they know how to describe the panic in the stock exchanges, the rush of bankruptcies, the ruined businesses, the suicides; books have been published which set out the figures of the new poverty.

But the figures are only a faltering expression of what the streets scream at the top of their voices, all these empty streets, frozen with terror. To cross a Paris main road, formerly swarming with people, and find yourself alone, listening to your own footsteps, feeling yourself spied upon, perhaps envied because you're wearing a new overcoat, to pass a café, and discover that it has just been protected with iron bars; to arrive at another one and find yourself having to whisper platitudes in the proprietor's ear; that was the climate of the century of Beatrice.

It did not take hold everywhere at the same time. Poverty took years to spread, like an epidemic with a lazy but indisputably contagious virus. People modified their way of life accordingly; many had barely enough to live on; those who had money to spend were ashamed to do so; in the large cities there was violence everywhere, rural areas became less and less welcoming.

The rumours of kidnappings were only a symptom of the evil. The watch on maternity homes, day nurseries and schools was strengthened; every day I thanked heaven that Beatrice had had a son; people who had daughters used to escort them everywhere, unremittingly; even adolescent girls had to be accompanied, preferably by more than one person.

All the governments of the North had to devote an increasing effort to security, but if the sight of these measures dissuaded certain individuals from committing crimes, they also reminded 'normal' people of the insecurity all around, and discouraged them from venturing into the streets.

So folk remained at home, to the great misfortune of shop-keepers, restaurant owners and people in the entertainment business. And in their own homes, what did people do? They watched on the TV screen the constant stream of pictures of daily violence, in their own town first of all, then in neighbouring regions, then the distant but haunting violence which continued without relaxation in the countries of the South.

This age of retrogression and weariness was – why should I speak of it in the past tense? it still is – an age of suspicion and a total hotchpotch of false ideas. The dark-skinned, the frizzy-haired, the foreigner seemed like the peripatetic carrier of violence. This has never been my view of things, and never will be. The woman I chose and loved, the daughter she gave me, the son-in-law I have welcomed and consider as my flesh and blood, all three belong to the brown-skinned nebula of migrants, and I myself, by alliance, by love, by conviction and by temperament, have always felt solidarity with them. But I would not have blamed my frightened neighbours. I do not despise their frightened shudders. And I take care not to argue with them; they have the apparent facts on their side. They feel themselves invaded by the world's misery, and by the resentment that misery brings with it, the vile impedimenta that certain migrants dare not discard.

What would I have said if people still listened? That our ancestors had their share of guilt? That we have our overwhelming share? That poverty is as bad a counsellor as wealth? That salvation must be for the whole planet or not at all? That . . .

But that language is no longer appropriate. When one is powerless against leprosy, one attacks the leper, one builds walls to quarantine him. Century-old wisdom, century-old folly.

Z

After what I have just written, dare I add that the miseries of the world have led me very nearly to the place where I wished to end up in?

Let me explain. Formerly, Clarence's idea of her retirement, our retirement, was an endless trip round the world. To recover from her frenzy of travelling, she thought that, rather than a sedentary existence, it would be good to set out for the same countries, but differently, more slowly, without watch or notebook, with no obligations, not even the obligation to enjoy herself, nothing but a succession of peaceful peregrinations.

Events occurred to cut short her dreams of the East, destroy her vision of the Tropics, escape was out of the question, partly because of her own state, but particularly because of the state of the planet.

At the time when her plans still had some meaning, Clarence used to talk them over with me, in the evening, when she had had a trying day. I let her wander on; then I would put my arm gently round her waist, as if we were taking a stroll together on the spot; with my head thrown back, I would gaze at her beaming face and just plant a kiss on her hair, which was scarcely turning silver, and her bare brown shoulders; for nothing in the world would I have blocked her field of vision.

And, naturally, I did not contradict her. Nevertheless, my idea of our retirement was quite different: hers was leisurely and nomadic, mine was studious and sedentary, a microscope in a barn in Savoy. But I would not have imposed this cloistered existence on my companion, I would first have followed her along the roads, then, with the help of age, she would have followed me to my cottage. Fate so willed it that we omitted one stage, hers.

For years my own dreams had had their home near the Alps; Clarence's came to join them there. Both of us longed now to live in this sort of observatory perched on the roof of Europe; perhaps, by thus moving far away, we might be able to preserve our lucidity, the ultimate dignity of ageing.

In the thirtieth year of the Century of Beatrice I transferred my library, my instruments, my collection of insects and my winter clothes to Les Aravis. The holiday resort was thereby established as a permanent home, for all the seasons that I still had to live.

By now I was finding the city intolerable. People clung to the walls, dark rings under eyes, dark glances; I imagine that was how it was during the Second World War, when nights were cold and coal was in short supply. But today it was neither war nor the cold. It was weariness. The taste of defeat without the excitement of war. Winter in your gut, that no fire can soothe.

People and streets were equally unrecognizable; sometimes I started to listen to my own thoughts. Fear gives birth to monsters.

My own fear was two-fold. As a city-dweller, I looked with suspicion on every unfamiliar face, every crowd; if only

I could, with one gesture, reduce to ashes all the passers-by whose shadows worried me . . . One winter evening, I saw a gang of youngsters at the corner of my street; they had lit a sort of bonfire on the pavement; it was crackling; formerly it would have amused me, I would have made some friendly remark to them; instead of which, I made a detour to avoid them and, before entering my building, I cast at them, from a distance, a baleful glance.

It was only when I had got home, after barricading the front door with its triple locks, that I gave way to my second fear, the fear of myself, of what the darkened city had done to me, fear and shame at the way I was now looking on my fellow-men and on the world.

I had to get away, urgently. I had to get away to find serenity. When I was protected from people, perhaps I would learn to love them again.

During this latter period, the only thing that attached me still to Paris was the presence of Beatrice, Florian and Morsi. If I had to save myself, it had to be with all my family.

Normally, I tend to let people, even those closest to me, follow their own bent; respect for others, even for their aberrations, has always been a religion for me. This time, however, I was determined to transgress. I became insistent, stirring up all my daughter's feelings of love and fear to force her into a decision. Morsi's own parents badgered him also with suggestions for jobs in Geneva for both himself and Beatrice; then they would only be less than an hour from Les Aravis. To my great relief, they eventually gave in. And it was only when they were all near me that I regained my taste for living and could get back to some work.

I had not yet planned to write this book as a record of events. The time that I did not devote to my family, I preferred to spend with my microscope and my collection of coleoptera. And if I occasionally came across a letter from André Vallauris in my files, or an article he had cut out or copied, I put it away in a drawer without lingering over it.

When exactly did I get the idea of acting as a chronicler? Perhaps, quite simply, the day I happened on a thick unused note-book with an alphabetical index, which I had acquired in the year Beatrice was born. I left it lying for several weeks on my table, without being able to make up my mind to get rid of it or put it away. Then, one day, I opened it, picked up a pen and began to write the first lines.

Soon, without a word to anyone, not even to Clarence – perhaps I was not sure until quite recently that I'd be able to complete a work so remote from what I did as an entomologist – I got into the habit of shutting myself up for hours on end and writing page after page, as I remembered things, simply letting myself be guided by the sequence of letters, from A to Z, to string the chapters together.

And now I have nearly reached the last full stop, and I feel myself gradually relieved of a burden, which I never suspected of being so heavy. Will this text ever be published? Will someone be found to take an interest in it? And in how many years time? That, I feel inclined to say, is no longer my problem. Whatever its fate, my role is over. When you cast a bottle into the sea, you naturally hope someone will fish it out; but you don't swim after it.

And then, at the present moment, I am not ashamed to admit, my sole concern is to shield my little tribe from the upheavals of the world, to protect them as far as possible from violence and despondency, and to keep a field in my tiny kingdom, at Les Aravis, where they can continue to enjoy life.

By dint of devoting countless days of my leisure to hard toil, my Savoyard retreat has become a most comfortable home; I see it as my Mount Ararat – the mountain in Armenia where Noah's Ark came to rest; fear rises over the world like the waters of the Flood, seeming perhaps a grandiose sight to those who remain on dry land.

Grandiose, how cynical this word seems! And yet, all tragedy is grandiose, every apocalypse is grandiose . . . But I have to say that I expected other fascinations, other excitements for this century of my old age.

How many times have I not asked myself how we got to this pass. In the preceding pages I have set out events, impressions, apparent causes. And now that I am preparing to quit the stage, without haste but without regret, I am still unable to say whether, at any given moment, the course of destiny could have been changed, and re-routed to bring it more into line with men's dreams. However often I re-read my chronicle, together with so many other accounts of these last years, I still remain perplexed. Was everything that happened unavoidable? I think not, I still believe that other paths existed . . .

I often think of those lost futures. Sometimes, as sunk in my daydreams I take my daily walk along the mountain paths, I go back sixty years, long before the beginning of the Century of Beatrice, and I try to imagine what different paths this irksome species to which I belong could have followed.

Then, in the space of one walk, I build a different world. A world in which freedom and prosperity have gradually spread like the waves on the surface of the waters. A world in which the only challenge left to medicine, after it has overcome all diseases and wiped out epidemics, is to postpone ageing and death indefinitely. A world from which ignorance and violence have been banished. A world rid of the last patches of darkness. Yes, mankind reconciled, generous and victorious, with eyes fixed on the stars, on eternity.

To that species, I would have been proud to belong.

One day soon, I shall not return from my walk. I know, I am waiting for this day, I scarcely fear it. I shall set out along some familiar path. My thoughts will frisk, out of control. Suddenly, exhausted by the effort to build my world, exhilarated, excited, my heart will begin to beat irregularly. I shall lean for support against some familiar oak tree.

There, in this state, a mixture of torpor and final serenity, I shall, for one brief moment, have the most precious illusion: the world, such as I knew it, will seem like an ordinary nightmare, and my dream-world will take on the appearance of reality. I shall begin to believe in it again, a little more every moment. That will be the world my eyes will embrace for the last time. A child's smile will illuminate my beard, that echoes the colour of the mountain. And I shall close my eyes, at peace.

LEO THE AFRICAN

Amin Maalouf

Leo the African is based on the true life-story of
Hasan al-Wazzan, the sixteenth-century traveller and writer
who came to be known as Leo Africanus, or Leo the African.

From his childhood in Fez, having fled the Christian Inquisition,
through his many journeys to the East as an itinerant merchant,
Hasan's story is a quixotic catalogue of pirates, slave-girls and
princesses, encompassing the complexities of a world in a state
of religious flux. Hasan too is touched by the instability of the
era, performing his *hadj* to Mecca, then converting to
Christianity, only to revert to the Muslim faith later in life.

In re-creating Hasan's extraordinary experiences, Amin
Maalouf sketches an irresistible portrait of the Mediterranean
world as it was nearly five centuries ago - the fall of Granada,
the Ottoman conquest of Egypt, Renaissance Rome under the
Medicis: all contribute to a background of spectacular colour,
matched only by the picaresque adventures of Hasan's life.

Vivid, gripping, and remarkable in its scope, *Leo the African* is
a masterpiece of the imagination from this award-winning writer.

'The most entertaining education we could wish for ... *Leo the
African* is a celebration of the romance and power of the Arab
world, its ideals and achievements'
Daily Telegraph

'Dazzlingly exotic'
Observer

Abacus
0 349 10600 2

THE ROCK OF TANIOS

Winner of the Prix Goncourt

Amin Maalouf

'A hugely impressive book, with things to admire on almost every page'
Sunday Telegraph

An exploration of myth, passion and loyalty from the Lebanon's
troubled past, *The Rock of Tanios* is another superbly rich and
rewarding novel from the author of *Samarkand* and *Leo the African*.
Expertly controlling his multi-faceted narrative with prose of
great beauty and power, Maalouf delves into the history of an
extraordinary life: the life of Tanios, child of the mountains.

'*The Rock of Tanios* is a compelling story of love, treachery and
murder, but it is far more complex than that ... passionate,
resonant and beautifully crafted. Needless to say, it is also
hugely engrossing ... Highly recommended'
Claire Messud in the *Guardian*

'He is a master storyteller ... and his observation of human
nature in all its facets is wonderfully accurate throughout'
David Robson in the *Sunday Telegraph*

'Asks all the questions pertinent to the post-colonial condition, but does
so with a languid readability that renders the didactic experience painless'
Giles Coren in *The Times*

Abacus
0 349 10662 2

SAMARKAND

Amin Maalouf

'An example of the best type of historical fiction'
Times Literary Supplement

Accused of mocking the inviolate codes of Islam, the Persian
poet and sage Omar Khayyam fortuitously finds sympathy
with the very man who is to judge his alleged crimes.
Recognising Khayyam's genius, the judge decides to spare
him and gives him instead a small blank book, encouraging
him to confine his thoughts to it alone ...

Thus begins the seamless blend of fact and fiction that is
Samarkand. Vividly re-creating the history of the manuscript
of the *Rubaiyaat* of Omar Khayyam, Amin Maalouf spans
continents and centuries with breathtaking vision: the
dusky exoticism of 11th-century Persia, with its poetesses
and assassins; the same country's struggles nine hundred
years later, seen through the eyes of an American academic
obsessed with finding the original manuscript; and the fated
maiden voyage of the *Titanic*, whose tragedy led to the
Rubaiyaat's final resting place - all are brought to life with
keen assurance by this gifted and award-winning writer.

'A remarkable novel ... Maalouf's descriptions of the courts, the
bazaar, the lives of mystics, kings and lovers are woven into an
evocative and languid prose ... an extraordinary book'
Independent

Abacus
0 349 10616 9

THE GARDENS OF LIGHT

Amin Maalouf

Born in a Mesopotamian village in the third century, the son of a Parthian warrior, Mani grows up in a volatile and dangerous world. As battle rages for control over the Middle East between the great Roman and Persian empires, as Jews and Christians, Buddhists and Zoroastrians fight for ascendancy, Mani – painter, mystic, physician and prophet – makes his way through the battlefields to preach his incandescent doctrine of humility, tolerance and love, a doctrine that comes to be known as Manicheanism.

A vivid glimpse of the ancient world in all its perfumed splendour and cruelty, an elegantly philosophical discourse on the fall of man, *The Gardens of Light* is a story of great beauty and resonance, exquisitely told.

'Amin Maalouf, who won the Prix Goncourt in 1993, weaves tapestries of intrigue that illuminate a broader historical moment ... in his engaging prose, [he] goes a considerable way towards restoring Mani to us ... Maalouf is as eloquent as ever'
Claire Messud, *The Times*

'A romantic and affectionate tale ... the history of Mani gains from the personal perspective of an author who knows the impact of sectarian hatreds too well ... engaging ... eloquent'
TLS

Abacus
0 349 10871 4